Sleep With Me

Jamie DeBree

Sleep With Me
ISBN 978-1-937477-58-5
Sleep With Me Copyright © 2013 Jamie M DeBree
Published by Brazen Snake Books
All rights reserved.

Edited by Carol R. Ward

Also by the Author

Tempest

Desert Heat

The Biker's Wench

The Minister's Maid

Indelibly Inked

Rock Me, Stalk Me

Heart Knocks

Chapter One

"Wine me, dine me, shag me...then leave. That's the deal."

Katherine knew she should smile or maybe flip her hair and bat her eyes, but the man she'd approached at the bar looked experienced enough to know what she was asking for. Voices murmured around them as she waited for the answer.

"Shag you?" he repeated, the corners of his lips curving up. "Does anyone actually say that anymore?"

She rolled her eyes. "It's better than the alternative. Are you in or not? Because I have a prescription to fill and I need to find a guy to fill it by tomorrow."

The man chuckled. "You have a prescription for sex? And any guy will do? Then why me?"

"Well...I find you physically attractive," Katherine said with a shrug. "And you also look like the kind of guy who doesn't mind a one-night stand, which is basically what we're discussing. I don't want an attachment, I don't need to find true love, and I don't need a guy who wants my number. I just want drinks, dinner and sex. Then we go our separate ways. But apparently I misjudged you, so I apologize for interrupting your evening."

She turned away, scanning the room for any other potentially suitable candidates. Who would have thought this assignment would be so difficult? Candace was so going to pay when she got home. Take a vacation, she'd said. Get laid. Nothing like a good orgasm to take care of that whole not-sleeping issue.

Right. Katherine wondered when her friend-slash-therapist had tried to get laid last. After being mistaken for a call girl twice and now turned down for...well, she wasn't exactly sure why she'd been rejected this last time...she was about ready to go back to her little bungalow on the beach and stay there for the rest of the week.

A jolt of awareness shot up her arm as warm fingers closed around her left wrist. Instinctively she pulled away, but her captor wouldn't let go. She looked down into her most recent target's amused emerald eyes.

"Hang on a sec," he said, finally releasing her wrist. "I didn't say I wouldn't do it, I just wanted to know why me. When were you thinking this little date would occur? And why drinking and dinner first, if all you want is sex?"

Katherine was all too aware that it had gotten quiet in the bar. Apparently their little conversation was garnering a lot of attention - something she really didn't want.

"You know what?" She moved a step back from the bar, keeping her wrists out of reach. "Forget it. It was a stupid idea. I'll...um...see you around. Or not. A girl can hope." She walked as quickly as she could while maintaining a cool facade to the front door and pushed out into the humid island evening. Slipping her shoes off, she hooked the straps with a finger and set off towards the beach.

She'd barely begun to feel the sand between her toes when her mystery man ran up beside her.

"Giving up so easily?" he asked, keeping pace as she kept walking. "Or just looking for a new pool to choose from?"

She rolled her eyes, doing her best to ignore the distinctly male scent that was far too enticing. "Why do you care? You made it pretty clear you were more amused than interested, so just forget I said anything. I withdraw the proposal. Leave me alone."

He chuckled, the warm sound sending an unwelcome tingle up her spine. "But then I wouldn't get to see the guy who finally agrees to...ah...fill your prescription. Who's your doctor, anyways? I think I could use a prescription like that."

Katherine stopped, letting out a long sigh as she watched the huge sun slip far too quickly below the horizon. She turned to the man beside her and frowned.

"What is your name?" she asked, irritated that she didn't already know.

He grinned, holding out his hand. "David Patton. And you are?"

"Katherine Gibson. Nice to meet you," she said automatically, reaching out to grasp his palm. She barely suppressing a gasp of awareness when her skin contacted his, and yanked her hand back before she could stop herself. The lights from the waterfront bars cast a dark orange glow over everything, but she could still see his amusement in the dim light.

"Listen David. You've had your fun, I've embarrassed myself and I don't know about you, but I'm tired. So I'm going back to my hut now. Alone. You have a good evening."

She brushed by him and continued on her way, hoping her burning cheeks had been mostly shadowed. Half-expecting him to show up at her side again, she was inexplicably annoyed when he didn't.

"Hey Kat!"

She cringed at the nickname she'd hated since grade school and kept walking.

"Meet me here tomorrow night at six," David called out. It was a statement, not a question, but that didn't surprise her from a guy like that. She considered it for a second before she yelled over her shoulder to him.

"Sorry, I'm busy. Thanks anyways though." With a small, hopefully dismissive wave she continued on down the beach to the hut she'd rented.

Once inside, she flopped down on the bed and wished she hadn't paid up front. The whole vacation had been Candace's idea, and her friend had pushed for the non-refundable advance payment option. Probably because she knew Katherine would be ready to leave after the first night.

Rolling over, she picked up the phone and dialed room service, ordering dinner for delivery. Maybe tomorrow she could find a tour to take or something interesting.

Something that didn't involve men.

* * * *

David watched the lanky brunette as she walked away, her curvy hips swaying as she pushed across the soft sand. If it was a baby she was after, she'd probably get it eventually with a body like that, though she didn't really strike him as the desperate-to-be-a-single-mom type. Maybe it was all part of the bigger plan for her. His monthly wage garnishment was proof that some women would do just about anything to have a baby - and she'd actually expected him to play daddy afterward too. No way was he falling for that shit again.

Still, there was something about Kat that intrigued him. Not enough to sleep with her, no matter how attractive she was in a bikini, but enough that he'd been willing to offer drinks. Maybe even dinner.

As she faded into the darkness he turned and went back to the bar. Thanks to Ms. Prescription-for-Sex, he was feeling a bit peckish himself. Luckily there were plenty of island girls who would be happy for his company with no desire for offspring. Or not his, at least.

The next morning, David wished he'd said no to that last shot of Jack. His head throbbed in time with the alarm clock, set only because he'd foolishly said yes when the resort asked him to lead the early snorkeling tour today. With the bright sunshine pouring into his eyes like battery acid, the extra money suddenly didn't seem worth the effort.

Dragging himself out of bed and into a pair of tight running shorts and a wet suit, he popped a few painkillers and grabbed his gear. Luckily it was a quick jaunt to the beach from his room behind the surf shop and he was only five minutes late to the boat. His partner, Amy Thomas looked pointedly at the big diving watch on her wrist.

Damn morning people.

"Nice of you to join us," she said with a faux cheer he was pretty sure she'd patented. "We're just waiting for one late sign-up. Otherwise I'd have left your ass behind."

He grinned. "You wouldn't leave me and we both know it. But I'll express my appreciation to the latecomer all the same. Hope she's cute."

Amy sneered. "I hope he's five-hundred pounds and hairy." Her gaze drifted over his shoulder, her brow furrowing. "Dammit. You really are the luckiest man alive, I swear. When you're done drooling, cut us loose so we can get going, okay?"

She walked away, leaving David to turn back toward the dock. His lips curved up in a welcoming smile as those long, slender legs from last night came into view.

"Well hello there, Kat. Didn't expect to be seeing you again so soon." He reached out to help her board, but she hung back, the expression on her face telling him the feeling was mutual.

She sighed, glancing back at the beach as if she'd like to run away. "What are *you* doing here? You really don't seem like a guy who likes mornings." She peered closer, lifting her dark glasses up to examine his eyes with a frown. "Your eyes don't either. Do they let you dive when you've been drinking? Because that doesn't really seem safe. Not that I care about your safety, or anything."

David recoiled, feigning surprise with a dramatic hand to his chest. "Oh come on - just because I won't sleep with you is no reason to be all insulting. Isn't it a bit too early for the claws, Kitty Kat?"

"Don't call me that!" she said, obviously fighting to keep from yelling. "My name is Katherine. Not Kat, not Kitty, not anything else. Just Katherine. Got it?" She put her hands on her hips, those gorgeous hazel eyes flashing.

He considered it for a second, and then shook his head as he stepped onto the dock and began untying the aft tether from the mooring.

"Sorry, I don't think I can remember that. Katherine is just too uptight. And while you may act that way, you definitely..." he slid his shades to the end of his nose and pointedly looked her up and down, "do not look like a woman who has reason to be uptight." Pushing his sunglasses back up, he finished untying the rope and tossed it onto the deck of the boat. Then he went back to the open gate in the railing and held out his hand to her.

"You'd better climb aboard if you're joining us. We're already late, Kitty Kat. Unless you'd let a little thing like contempt for yours truly stop you from experiencing some of the most beautiful sight-seeing the ocean has to offer..."

* * * *

Katherine wanted to leave. She wanted it so badly it took all of her strength to ignore the hand her nemesis extended, grasp the boat railing and carefully step over the small space between the dock and the deck, sealing her fate for the next several hours.

"You don't happen to know where I can find the person in charge, do you?" she finally called out as he untied another rope and tossed it onto the boat. There were a lot of empty seats in the sunken area to her left, although several bags were lying randomly on the decking. Maybe she'd found the wrong boat by accident. There were probably other snorkeling trips going out at the same time. The thought brightened her mood, however slightly.

David laughed. "Why? Gonna try to have me left behind?"

Katherine sighed. "I actually hadn't thought of that, though it's not a bad idea. But I should check in and make sure I'm in the right place. I signed up late - I never do that but I couldn't sleep anymore and the water looked nice and my...uh, Candace said I should--" she clamped her mouth shut, frowning. Why on earth was she telling him all this?

Stupid. He was making her stupid. She should just go, and schedule a trip for another day. Ahead. Like sane people did.

"Never mind." She moved to step back over to the dock, but he was blocking her path. "I'm just going to go. I'll take another tour later. I need to just...go." Her heart race sped up slightly as he braced an arm on either side of the metal railing and she was effectively trapped. This wasn't right. She should be able to check in. Where was the instructor? Where were the other tourists? What if David was actually a...no, that was stupid. She just needed to go back to the hotel and relax. Attractive, handsome men always messed with her head. And her body.

Damn, he smelled good. Why did he have to smell good?

He shook his head, and then took off his shades again, looking a little too closely at her face for comfort. His expression grew serious, and his concern was almost palpable.

"Hey - are you afraid of boats? Or water? The instructor for this trip is me, and if you've got a phobia I need to know now."

Katherine closed her eyes and took a deep breath in, letting it out slowly. Which didn't really help since his scent was inescapable at this proximity.

A light touch on her arm shocked her out of her trance. She pulled away, lost her balance and two seconds later she found herself flat on the deck as David ran to kneel at her side.

"Are you okay? I didn't mean to scare you, I just thought you might pass out or something. Did you hit your head?"

She took stock silently for a moment before sitting up, heat rising in her face. "I'm fine," she said, feeling a deep rumble vibrate into a low growl beneath her. "What is that noise?"

"The engine." David helped her to her feet, looking slightly wounded as she pulled her hand away as quickly as possible. Didn't he know how electric his skin was?

"I'm afraid you're stuck with me now, but if you're afraid of water or anything like that, tell me now and you can just stay on the boat. This isn't the place or time to be working through your fears. You need a shrink for that."

Katherine gave him a small sarcastic laugh. "I'm not afraid, okay? I just really need to be organized, is all. I go a little nuts when things don't go as planned."

Or when a super-hot jerk is within fifty yards.

"Ah," he said, as if she'd just revealed the key to unlock all the secrets of the universe. "That explains...a lot. Well," he turned toward the cabin, pointing at a figure inside. "That's Amy - she's our captain for this trip, and will stay with the boat at all times. The other tourists are up front - people normally start up there so they can watch for wildlife and just see where we're going. It will be half an hour or so until we get to the reef. I'll go over instructions back here in fifteen minutes. The dive schedule is on the cabin wall to your left. And even if I wanted to, I can't predict what will happen once we're in the water, but most people seem to have more fun when they relax and go with the flow."

With that, he walked off toward the front of the boat.

She watched him go, the murmur of voices finally penetrating her consciousness as her panic slowly subsided. Taking advantage of the quiet, she took a seat in the lower area and took a water bottle out of her bag, taking a long sip before replacing it.

Watching the waves go by, she reflected on the discussion that had started this whole mess. Candace, her best friend from college had just opened up her own psychology practice. Plagued by insomnia for the past two months, Katherine had jokingly asked for a prescription, and Candace had very seriously recommended a vacation that completely deviated from her normal routines, and sex. She even backed it up with some psychological study that was dulled further by the bottle of wine they were sharing. Katherine had laughed off the idea at first, but as her insomnia got worse and fatigue started affecting both her work and home life, desperation sent her to Candace's travel agent.

She'd literally begged for a trip to somewhere with sandy beaches and hot, easy men. It wasn't a moment she was proud of.

She took another sip of water and shook her head in frustration. The irony was, it wasn't even working. She'd been on the tiny island she couldn't even remember the name of for two nights and two and a half days. So far, it seemed as though the men were either indifferent or jerks, and even serenaded by the sea and island breezes at night, she still couldn't sleep more than a couple hours at a time.

As if on cue, she yawned, quickly covering her mouth with one hand as the other people in the group began shuffling back to join her in the seating area. David was at the back of the group, and didn't even seem to notice her as he took his place in front of them near the cabin.

She only half-listened to his instructions, her mind soothed by the low timbre of his voice mixed with the rumble of the motor. Maybe if she hired him to just drive her around on the ocean all night, she could get some decent rest...

Chapter Two

David finished his standard scuba diving lecture and glanced over at Kat as the rest of the group began to get ready. She appeared to be sleeping, her eyes closed and her face more peaceful than he'd seen it yet. He vaguely remembered her saying something about not sleeping well the night before. Maybe if he let her sleep, she'd be in a better mood when they got back to the dock.

Then Amy cut the engine and Kat's eyes popped open, blinking and confused until one of the teens who was disregarding David's instructions and slapping around the deck in his flippers slapped a fin across both of Kat's feet.

David cringed, watching as her eyes widened in shock before she pulled her feet up on the seat and wrapped a hand around each one, squeezing hard. He expected a string of expletives or worse, but she simply lowered her forehead to her knees.

"Sorry!" the teen yelled before turning and laughing with his friends as if nothing happened. David glanced over at the parent, who merely shrugged.

Some days, the job sucked.

"Hey," David said, pitching his voice loud enough to be heard over the laughter. He walked over to the teens, standing in front of the one who'd hurt Kat. "What did I say about fins on before we dive?"

The kid shrugged, but his smile faded.

"Take them off now, or you stay on the boat. Your choice."

The rest of the group quieted down as the dad spoke up.

"Come on, man - they were just having fun. And he apologized. Cut 'em a break?"

David shook his head and walked over to where Kat was still curled in a ball.

"Do you know how much damage you can do to someone with those on land?" He reached down and gently pried her fingers off of one foot, revealing the angry purple welt rising over the top of it. "Not only does this hurt - a lot - but Kat's going to have a hard time wearing her own fins now to dive. All because you were 'just having fun'." He reluctantly let go of Kat's foot.

"So no, I'm not going to cut them, or anyone on this boat, a break. The rules are in place not just for your safety, but the safety of everyone else too. If you won't follow them on the boat, I can't trust you to follow them underwater, and people die when that happens. Got it?"

The dad nodded, along with most of the others and the teen sat down with his friends, removing his fins. David glanced back at the cabin and saw Amy standing in the doorway with a roll of water proof tape and some gauze in hand, fighting a grin. She was always amused when he had to be the bad guy, for some reason. Probably because he normally made her do it.

Since she was so amused, he decided she could get everyone set to go in.

"Listen up, people. Captain Amy is going to get you situated to go in the water now. Remember the rules we discussed, and if you have any questions at all, ask her before you get wet. I'll be with you shortly."

He walked over to Amy and handed her the clipboard with partner assignments, taking the tape and gauze.

"Smooth," she said in a low voice. "Think that was enough to get on her good side? Because from what I overheard earlier, she's not all that fond of you."

He grinned. "Aw, come on Amy. All women warm up to me eventually. Even you, and you don't even like men. Now go get those people in the water while I try not to get scratched."

She shook her head and gave him a dubious look. "Good luck with that," she said, walking away with the clipboard.

Kat was examining her marred feet when he sat down beside her.

"Still sting pretty bad?" he asked.

She nodded, not looking up. "I'm not sure how I'm going to get those fins on," she said, her voice breaking slightly. "It's right under where the top of the fin should hit, and--"

"I think I can help with that. A little gauze and some tape..." he waited for her to look up. Except she didn't. He examined the side of her face more closely, saw her eyelashes flutter as she blinked hard.

Damn.

"It's okay if you want to stay here," he said, not really sure what to do. Crying had never been something he was equipped for. "You can keep Amy company, and we'll sign you up for another trip when your feet feel better. No charge, of course."

Katherine nodded, too embarrassed to speak. Her feet hurt, but that wasn't the only reason she didn't want to go. Blinking again to hold back the stupid tears, she wished for the millionth time that she'd stayed home. At home, everything was within her control. Her schedule was set, and when she did deviate from it, there was a good reason and it wasn't for long.

This whole vacation thing was just a horrible failure. It hurt that of all the things she could control, relaxing and having fun wasn't one of them. Thank God it would all be over in a couple more days.

She swallowed, taking a breath and letting it out slowly before she finally looked over at David.

"Thank you," she said, forcing her lips into a half-smile. "I appreciate that. I'll wait here."

He seemed relieved and smiled back as he stood up. "We'll be out for an hour, so it won't be too long. Don't believe anything Amy says about me, okay?"

Katherine raised her eyebrows, but wasn't in the mood to spar with him. "Okay."

His smile faded and he left, leaving her feeling like a heel. She watched as he tapped Amy on the shoulder and then took the clipboard as the captain came in her direction.

"Let me know if you need anything," she said as she passed by. "There's water in that cooler over there. I'll be in the cabin."

Katherine nodded as the woman walked by. Apparently she wasn't a talker, and that was fine with Katherine. Some alone time would probably do her a lot of good. Maybe she could even nod off again for awhile.

After the group had disappeared behind the boat, Katherine closed her eyes and laid her head back against the seat. The sun was warm, the breeze light, and the sound of the water lapping gently against the boat lulled her into the restful state between sleep and awareness. Images of clear water and brightly colored corals played behind her eyes, curious fish dancing in front of her mask as she floated with the current. Consciousness was slipping peacefully away until several dull thuds rudely snapped her back to reality.

Opening her eyes, she blinked against the bright sun and surveyed the boat deck. Near the back, someone in full scuba gear was preparing to enter the water. A blond ponytail swinging back and forth was enough to identify the ship's captain.

Flexing her feet, Katherine realized they didn't really hurt anymore. There was no way she could catch up to the group, but maybe she could tag along with Amy for awhile. Surely that would be safe. And probably more fun than worrying about David watching her too.

Standing up, she called out, waving as she tried to get Amy's attention, to no avail. Quickly stripping out of the wrap dress she'd put on over her suit that morning, she got the fins and mask they'd assigned her and hurried to the launch area at the back of the boat, but Amy had already disappeared below the water. A little ways off, bubbles surfaced from her tanks, and Katherine hurried to put on her fins and mask, fit the snorkel in her mouth and lower herself into the shockingly cool water.

All of the sound and chaos from above was immediately muted when she put her head underwater. It was a whole different world full of amazing colors that exceeded anything her imagination could come up with, though it looked deeper than she'd expected. Glancing in the direction of those bubbles, she could just barely make out Amy's figure, farther away than she'd originally thought. Making sure to keep her strokes even and slow as David had coached them to avoid scaring the wildlife, Katherine began to move toward Amy's position, staying beside the coral but careful not to touch it. If she didn't catch up soon, she'd go back to the boat, but she'd enjoy the view for a few minutes, at least.

* * * *

David hoisted himself out of the water, doing a quick head count to make sure everyone was back on the boat before glancing toward the seating area. Frowning when he didn't see Kat, he noted Amy's wet scuba gear sitting off to the side but didn't see either woman anywhere on the deck. As the rest of the group filed back into the main area of the boat, he went to the cabin, raising an eyebrow when he passed the dress Kat had been wearing earlier on a bench.

Had Amy managed to seduce a customer? Kat sure didn't seem at all interested in women, but sometimes it was hard to tell. He wasn't sure whether he should be impressed or just mad that Amy had horned in on his action.

Knocking on the cabin door, he let himself in to hear Amy broadcasting on the ship-to-shore radio.

"That's correct," she said, her calm voice belying the concerned look on her face. "It can't have been more than half an hour - I was out for fifteen minutes, and she was gone when I got back. I'm trying to activate the GPS tracker in her fins now."

David's heart rate spiked as he realized what she was talking about. "What the hell happened? Where's Kat?"

Amy muted the microphone. "I don't know where she is, David. She was sleeping, I made a quick dive to check on the anchor chain because it seemed like it was dragging, and when I got back, she was gone. Her fins & mask are gone too. She must have thought she could catch up to you guys."

"You didn't see her? Why did you leave her up here alone?" He ran to the equipment panel and peered at a screen to the right. "Why don't we have her coordinates yet?"

Amy shook her head. "I'm not sure. It should be working. I've been scanning the immediate area for about five minutes, and...nothing."

"Damn it. She's not stupid, Amy - she wouldn't just go in alone. She was probably following you, and we need to find her as soon as possible. Where exactly did you go?"

"I just told you - I was checking on the anchor--"

David shook his head. "Don't fucking lie to me, Amy. Not now. Her *life* is in danger, and we both know you've been away from the boat while I'm out more than once." At her shocked look, he nodded. "That's right, I know. I saw you going over the reef when Pete and I were both out last week. So don't give me anymore crap - where the hell were you?"

She bowed her head, and David barely refrained from wrapping his fingers around her neck while he waited. Finally, her shoulders dropped and she sighed.

"Toward the island," she said finally, pointing to what appeared to be a large rock with a few trees growing out of it sticking up just to the west. "I went just to the other side of the reef and came right back. If she'd been behind me, I would have seen her one way or the other. Especially since she'd have to stay near the surface."

He shook his head, and checked the tracker screen again. "We need to get closer to the reef. She would have been drawn in by the colors and fish. Or that's what we have to hope. Pull up the anchor and get as close as you can. Then we'll see if her signal comes up. Did you call it in to the coast guard?"

"Not yet," Amy said, flipping a few switches on the control panel. "I was hoping we'd have a signal from her by now. I'll radio now."

Gears rumbled as they drew the anchor up and the boat's main engine came to life. Voices rose outside as Amy got on the radio, and David went to check on their guests and let them know about the delayed return to shore.

When he stepped out of the cabin, his heart skipped a beat at the sight of a body twitching on the deck, the view obscured by the other customers standing and kneeling around it. A quick scan made him realize that one of the teen boys was missing.

"Move aside, please. Let me through." He pushed people back so he could confirm it was the other teen. His dad was holding his head and David spread out his arms, motioning for everyone to move away from the flailing limbs.

"He's epileptic." The father looked up, a worried expression on his face. "His new medication's been working so well, the doctor said this trip should be okay. I never thought--"

"It's okay. Let's just focus on keeping him safe until it's over." David knelt beside the boy as the jerking started to subside, helping his father turn him to his side when he vomited.

Once the boy was calm, they made sure he was breathing okay and David helped move him to a makeshift bed of cushions on the deck.

"He needs to get to a hospital," the father said. David nodded, glancing out at the blue horizon.

"I know. Let me check with Amy and see how close the coast guard is. If they're still a ways out, I'll have her take you back in."

The man frowned. "Aren't we leaving anyway? I thought the trip was over."

"The woman who stayed behind is missing, and we need to find her." David held up a hand at the man's angry look. "Your son takes precedence right now, so please don't panic. I promise that we'll get him to shore as fast as possible, whether that's on this boat or with the coast guard. Just let me check with Amy and I'll know more, okay?"

The man shook his head. "Fine. But one way or the other, my son needs medical attention. If that woman was stupid enough to wander off on her own in the ocean..."

Strong hands grasped David's arms from behind, pulling him back before he could act on the urge to punch the guy's face.

"We'll be leaving within the next two minutes to get your son help, Sir," Amy said, moving between them. "Is there anything we can get for him in the meantime?"

The man looked down at his son, moving groggily on the cushions. He shook his head.

"Not until he's more aware."

Amy nodded. "Let me know if there's anything you need." She turned back to David. "I need to talk to you. Now." Pointing him toward the cabin, she gave him a shove and followed him inside, closing the door.

"There's no one out here today," she said without preamble. "There was a shark spotted off the main island, so they're clearing the beach over there, and apparently a yacht is sinking somewhere south so there's a rescue operation going on for that too. The closest boat is still docked, but they're heading out now. It will take half an hour for them to get here, and that kid--"

"I know, I know." David shook his head, thumping the equipment panel. He thought for a moment, and then turned to the door.

"Help me lower the dinghy," he said, grabbing an extra flashlight and a red plastic wrapped emergency tote from under the leeward counter. "I'll get my gear and head for the lagoon. If she stayed with the tide, it will have carried her over the reef. With any luck, she'll have headed for shore when she figured out she was lost."

"What if she didn't? What if she's already--"

David shook his head. "Don't. Just don't." He went out the door to the back of the boat and started unhooking the cables holding the dinghy in place, all too aware of the stares from their customers. He put the extra supplies and his scuba gear in and then lowered it down to the water with Amy's help.

"Where are you going?" a woman called out. "What about us?"

"Amy's going to take you back to the dock," he called, stepping down into the smaller boat. "I'm going to stay and wait for the coast guard. We can't leave Kat out here alone."

Looking at Amy, he lowered his voice. "If I don't come back with the coast guard, it's because I ended up on the island. Pick me up tomorrow night on the south end around sunset, okay?"

She nodded, then shoved the dinghy away from the ship as he started up the outboard motor. Keeping the throttle low, he turned the boat and headed slowly toward the reef, scanning the water and hoping for a miracle.

* * * *

Katherine reminded herself for the tenth time not to panic. Or was it the twentieth? She'd followed Amy's bubbles out over the center of the coral where it was much shallower than where the boat was, but there had been a few small sharks and a couple long, mean-looking fish to watch out for and when she'd finally looked forward again, the bubbles and the dim diver's outline were gone.

Knowing she should go back to the boat, she'd lifted her head out of the water to locate it, turning circles until she finally saw it bobbing what seemed like a much longer distance away than she'd realized. When she'd finally put her head back down to swim for it, there were more sharks circling. Reef sharks, she thought David had said, and supposedly harmless, but they were still big enough to make her nervous. Too late she realized that her frantic kicking when she was looking for the boat must have made them curious.

With considerable effort, she forced herself to slow her movements and drift over the reef with lazier kicks. No way was she leaving the relative shallow water on top of the reef with a bunch of sharks following though, so she swam along the top of the reef until they appeared to get bored and dissipated.

Careful to keep her movements rhythmic, she peeked above the water line again, shivering as she looked for the boat to reorient herself.

But it appeared to be gone. She couldn't see it no matter which way she turned, and her heart raced at the thought of being stranded alone in the vast ocean.

She never should have left the boat.

There was an island in the other direction, and after one more survey of the open sea with no sign of a boat or any human life at all, she decided her only chance was to swim for shore. It looked like an impossible distance, but if she got far enough, hopefully the tide would pull her in. And the island shouldn't move, which was a bonus.

She wished she could rest, maybe take a few good deep breaths, but having seen all the activity below the surface, she wasn't comfortable keeping her head up for any longer than necessary. She needed to see, to make sure nothing was coming after her. Forewarned is forearmed, or whatever that saying was.

Breathing as slowly as she could through the snorkel, she went horizontal again and started back across the coral fields with strong but steady strokes of her fins. No longer concerned with scaring the wildlife, she focused on moving as fast as possible without attracting undue attention. By the time she reached the inner edge of the reef, her legs were burning from the effort and she barely noticed the cold. But the drop-off ahead gave her pause even though she could still see the bottom, and it wasn't nearly as dark as the side she'd just left.

Lifting her head, she was relieved to see the island still sticking up out of the water. For a moment she'd feared having turned around and gone the opposite direction. Trembling as the cold worked its way back under her skin, she knew she needed to keep moving. The deeper water was disconcerting though, and she had to force herself to float out away from the apparent safety of the reef top.

She couldn't seem to warm up again as she swam over the sandy bottom. The wildlife didn't seem to mind her presence - in fact, she wished they would mind a little more. Several rays joined her for awhile, flying gracefully under her with gentle flaps and all she could think of was that animal guy on TV who had died swimming with rays. Long, skinny eels slithered partially out of rocky homes and watched her go by with sharp, gleaming white teeth. Fish of all shapes and colors darted around and below her, and her pulse raced as she tried to remember which of them were potentially dangerous.

Her lungs felt like they were going to burst, and so did her thighs. Shivers racked her body as her pace faltered. Her kicks grew more erratic, and that just made her pulse beat faster, knowing all sorts of dangerous creatures could sense her struggle.

The water grew choppy as the sand rose higher, and she finally gave in and flipped to her back, floating motionless in the tide.

Chapter Three

Skimming over the wide reef top, David fought the urge to go faster. He guided the boat in a zigzag pattern parallel to the shore before heading in toward the natural lagoon between the coast and the inland side of the reef. Kat was smart. She wouldn't have gone further out into open water if she had any choice in the matter - she would have tried for the island. It was a long swim even for a strong swimmer, so her chances weren't good, but if she could manage to stay afloat she might be able to ride in with the tide.

Taking note of the direction the currents were moving, he moved with them as he criss-crossed the lagoon toward the shore. He checked his watch - it had been a little over an hour since she'd gone missing. It wasn't a long time to be in the water, but considering how far she might have gone and what her mental state might be, it was still too long.

As he approached the beach, he scanned the sandy coast but it was empty. He started a new search grid moving farther down, assuming he'd underestimated the current. He went out to the reef and back again, but there was still no sign of her, and the dinghy only had enough gas for one more trip out if they needed to get to the coast guard ship.

He ignored the niggling voice in his head telling him the search was futile, and pulled the boat up onto the beach, intending to walk and watch the coastline. If she'd made it far enough in, the tide should wash her up on shore eventually. He just hoped she'd be alive when it did.

A flash of hot pink caught his eye in the water fifty yards down from where he stood. The island was deserted as far as he knew, so unless it was a tropical flower of some sort, there was a good chance it could be Kat. He grabbed the emergency bag from the boat and sprinted down the beach. Definitely human now that he was closer, the body rolled up and down with the gentle waves as it descended toward the beach.

Kat. It had to be, considering it wasn't a popular tourist destination, which made it the perfect spot, usually.

Wading out with a feeling of dread in his stomach, he finally grasped her under the arms and pulled her the rest of the way to shore. She didn't move or struggle at his touch, and he feared the worst as he dragged her high up on the warm sand.

Prying the snorkel out of her mouth, he removed the mask as gently as he could, relieved at the slow rise and fall of her chest. Feeling the side of her neck with two fingers, he pressed in until he felt a strong, steady pulse.

She stirred restlessly, her brow wrinkling and her head moving side to side. Quickly checking her over for injuries, he pried off her fins and checked the heel compartment for the GPS tracker chip.

It was missing.

"Am I dead?"

Her voice was groggy and weak, her eyes blinking rapidly against the bright afternoon sun. David moved to kneel at her head, shading her face with his body.

"Nope. But you are incredibly lucky. And stupid too, but we'll talk about that later. How are you feeling?"

Her body trembled visibly, and she brought her arms up over her chest, hugging herself. Her flesh prickled as the shivering grew more violent.

"D-d-dead," she mumbled through her chattering teeth. "F-f-freezing."

David got the emergency bag and opened it, taking out a chamois and a rolled up blanket.

"You're in shock. We need to get you dried off and out of this breeze so you can warm up. Your suit should dry pretty fast in the heat - I'm just going to try to soak up the extra water, okay?"

She nodded and he pressed the chamois over her suit, wringing it out over the sand and then repeating the action over her torso. Then he wiped down the rest of her body and got as much water out of her hair as possible before wrapping her in the blanket. He pulled her up to sit between his legs, her back leaning against his chest so she could soak up his body heat as the sun warmed her front.

The fact that she didn't argue was concerning, given what he'd experienced of her personality. Instead she seemed to sink into him, pressing for as much contact as possible with her face nestled against his neck. He held her close as the shivering began to subside, scanning the ocean for signs of the Coast guard ship that should be arriving any time.

He checked his watch twenty minutes later when there was still no sign of rescuers. Kat stirred, looking up at him from where she'd slid down to rest her head on his chest.

"Welcome back," he said as she reached up to rub her eyes. "That was a bit longer than the swim I'd planned today. How are you feeling?"

She started to push up on one elbow and he cringed until she apparently realized just where it was in relation to his anatomy. Her cheeks blushed red as she moved to a less damaging position before sitting up.

"I didn't think I was going to make it." She looked out at the sea, her expression tired and frustrated when she turned back to him.

"That was quite possibly the stupidest thing I've ever done in my life, and I'm sorry you had to come after me. I don't know what on earth I was thinking to leave the boat without Amy knowing I was following her."

David shrugged, uncomfortable with this nicer version of the spitfire he'd met last night.

"If I remember right, last night you were looking for a one-night stand. Seems like I'm destined to keep you out of trouble, now doesn't it?" He grinned, relieved to see her eyes flash fire again.

"Only a total jerk would bring that up right now." She shook her head and moved farther away, clutching the blanket around her. "And I don't need anyone taking care of me. I can take care of myself."

He raised his eyebrows.

"Well, usually. This isn't normal. This whole vacation was a really bad idea. And I appreciate you coming after me, so thank you. Now if you'll just take me back to the boat so we can get back to the main island, I'll stay out of your hair until my plane leaves."

David wrinkled his nose. She wasn't going to like this.

"The boat's gone," he said, deciding to just get it out there. "The kid who mashed your feet had a seizure on the deck, and they had to go back. I brought the rescue dinghy out to look for you." He pointed down the beach.

"The coast guard was supposed to be here to help me search and hopefully take us back by now, but I haven't seen their boat yet. So we're stuck here either until they show up, or until tomorrow night when I told Amy to come get me if I wasn't back today."

Kat looked at him in disbelief. "So what you're saying is that we are actually stranded on this island. What are we going to do about food? And clothes? Why can't we just take the small boat back?"

David laughed. "There isn't enough gas - and even if there was, it's not meant for that kind of distance travel. As for food..." he rummaged through the emergency bag and handed her a meal replacement bar. "We'll start a fire and catch some fish for dinner. With all these trees, I'm betting there's fresh water somewhere inland, though we can drink the coconut milk too. We'll be okay until Amy shows up."

Kat took the bar and ripped the package open, her face scrunching up when she took a bite.

"Ugh. We might starve to death if we have to eat more of these."

He laughed, rising to his feet and holding out a hand to help her up.

"Come on. If you're up for it, let's explore a little and see if we can find some fresh water and firewood. Then I'll catch us something a bit tastier for dinner."

* * * *

Katherine followed David up the beach until the sand gave way to gravel and dirt. Surveying the ground, she tried to find the smoothest path into the island forest, but it was rocky and sharp in every direction.

"Um, David?"

He turned around and raised his eyebrows, waiting.

She looked down, rocking back on her bare heels and wiggling her toes.

"I don't have any shoes."

He came back, looking at her feet. "I should have grabbed your clothes before I came looking for you. Will you be okay here by yourself while I get some wood? You could go down by the boat and wait there - we'll flip it on its side for shelter tonight."

She thought about it for a minute and nodded. "It would probably be good for someone to watch for the coast guard anyways, right?"

It was clear by his expression that he didn't think the coast guard would show up, but he nodded anyway.

"Absolutely. Why don't you take the emergency pack and your snorkel gear down there, and I'll be back as soon as I can. If you want to try fishing, there's some gear in the boat..."

Katherine shook her head, holding up both hands. "Sorry, but I'm not going anywhere near the water again today. I'll take our stuff back to the boat but that's it. You can fish when you get back."

"Okay then. I'll see you later. Holler if you need anything - I won't go far."

Katherine watched as he walked into the trees, tamping down the panic that tried to take hold. Staying anywhere alone seemed like a bad idea, but so did cutting her feet on the rocky terrain. Turning, she gathered up her gear and the bag he'd brought and started walking through the warm sand toward the small boat he'd left up the beach. When she reached it, she understood why going back to the main island wasn't really an option.

No bigger than a rowboat, there was really only room for six people, and that was if everyone squeezed together on the three slender benches spanning the aluminum craft. Wooden oars lay lengthwise on the bottom, and a small motor was perched on the back. A few thin metal boxes hung on the inside walls, presumably the fishing supplies David had referred to and the one with a large red cross on it undoubtedly held minor first aid supplies.

Dropping the bag and her gear in the sand, she rummaged through the supplies, taking stock of what they had and hoping it would be enough. There were several soft packages labeled drinking water, and she opened one with no small measure of guilt nagging at her as she poured it down her throat. She'd regret it later if the island didn't have a spring, but her throat had been so dry, her lips parched and cracking.

One of the metal containers revealed a bottle of sunscreen, and she spread a thin layer over all of the skin she could reach in hopes of preventing any further damage until the sun went down. Then she started looking around for something, anything that might be suitable temporary footwear.

Cutting down the fins would be the easiest solution, though she hesitated. Without them, she never would have reached the island, and if she ended up in the water again they would be essential. Then again, she didn't have any plans to swim again, and odds were good that if she did get wet, it wouldn't be because she meant to. So she wouldn't have the fins then anyway.

She'd have to risk it.

There was a large knife in the container where she'd found the sunscreen, and she used it to score a line on each flipper just beyond the end of the foot pocket. Working slowly, she cut into the thick rubber, thankful that the knife was sharp and sliced through the material easily. When they were both finished, she tugged the makeshift shoes on her feet and stood.

"Very stylish."

She looked up to see David jogging toward her, examining her new footwear.

She held up a foot, turning it side to side. "I know the fins might have come in handy, but it seemed like protecting my feet might be more important - especially if we need to go for water. I hope you don't mind. I'll pay for them when we get back."

He shook his head. "Don't worry about it. You're right, we will need to hike for water, so it's good you thought of it. I found a spring back in the trees, and there's a cave we can use for shelter. I just need to pull the boat up higher so it doesn't get pulled out by the tide, and I'll show you."

Katherine nodded. "Sounds good. What can I do to help?"

He went to the other side of the boat and gestured to the edge. "Grab that side and pull. It's not too heavy."

She pulled with him, not sure she was really helping any as the boat slid up the sand toward the trees and her feet slid down farther with each step. When he finally decided it was high enough, she gathered up their meager supplies while he tied a rope from the boat to a nearby tree, just in case.

"This way," he said, setting off into the jungle. Katherine was struck by the difference after just a few steps into the darker environment. The constant roar of the waves was muted, and everything seemed so much quieter as she followed David deeper. Gorgeous flowers bloomed in random places, even in trees, and everything was green and lush, but almost too quiet.

It wasn't long before she heard water running again. Emerging into a small clearing, she saw the stream and a slender waterfall that fell over the rock face he'd mentioned.

"It's beautiful," she said, amazed at how clear the water was. Ferns and other tropical bush-like plants grew along the banks, and thick vines hung down the cliffs, sporting bright flowers and thick, fleshy leaves.

David nodded. "I thought you'd like it. The cave is just over here. I built a fire pit earlier, so we just need to start a fire."

She followed him to the shallow depression in the cliffs and handed him the lighter she'd found in the metal kit on the boat. As the flames crackled to life, she realized just how cold she still was, and knelt down by the pit, holding her hands out to warm them.

David rummaged around behind her and a few minutes later, the blanket settled around her shoulders. She pulled it closer around her as he rubbed her arms gently.

"Getting warmer?" he asked, his voice taking on a low, sensual quality that she was sure she only imagined.

She nodded. "I think so. Thank you."

He was close - so close she couldn't seem to think about anything else. She wasn't sure whether she wanted him to take her in his arms and tell her everything would be okay, or move away before she did something completely stupid, like ask him to.

He released her, standing up and moving to the side where she could see the odd look on his face and the fishing pole he held in one hand. He must have put it together when he was getting the blanket. She wasn't sure she was ready to know what the look was about.

He gestured vaguely toward the stream, an old-style canteen hanging from his shoulder. "I'm going to catch us some dinner and get water. I shouldn't be long - that stream is hopping with fish." Without waiting for a response, he turned and walked away.

* * * *

By the time David had finished catching and cleaning two fish, dusk was settling over the jungle. He found a couple of forked branches and a longer one to go between and carried them with the fish back to the cave. Kat had been rummaging through the emergency pack, and set out the second blanket as well as a couple of empty coconut shells she'd found nearby, and she was setting more wood on the fire.

"You caught some!" She smiled, a hungry expression on her face.

"You sound surprised." Chuckling, he laid the fish on a flat rock while he set up the makeshift spit.

Kat shrugged, watching as he skewered each fish on the longer branch and hung them over the fire.

"I've never been fishing. It doesn't seem like it would be that easy to get a fish to bite a hook."

David turned the branch as dinner sizzled in the heat. "It's not about the hook - more about the bait. Feed them what they want, and you've got dinner." He handed her the canteen, and she poured a little into the coconut shells for each of them before setting it aside.

Kat nodded, watching quietly as he tended the meal. She was quiet, an uncommon trait in women as far as he knew. Most of them would fill the silence with endless chatter. He'd never met one who didn't. It was...disconcerting.

"So why do you want to have a kid?"

He wished he could take the question back the second it came out. It was none of his business, and judging from the look on Kat's face, she was about to make that abundantly clear.

"Why would you think I do? And why would you care if I did?" She raised her eyebrows, waiting. He knew that look. She wasn't waiting for an honest answer, she was waiting to rip him to shreds.

He held up both hands in surrender. "You're right, it's none of my business. I apologize. And I think..." he poked at one of the fish with his finger, "this is done. Let's eat."

Glancing at the surrounding foliage, he cut two large leaves off of a bushy plant of some sort and laid one fish on each, handing her one. Noting her watchful eye, he used his fingers to pull the skin off and then pieces of flesh, leaving the bones behind. She mimicked his movements in silence, her body tense as she picked the carcass clean.

"Thank you," she said quietly, wrapping the leaf around the bones. "What do we do with these?"

He took it from her and stood. "I'll toss 'em back in the stream. Hand me the canteen and I'll fill it up while I'm at it."

She wrinkled her nose. "You're going to put bones in the water and then we're going to drink it?"

"You know these fish came from the same water we're drinking, right? Besides, the bones will go downstream, and I'll fill the canteen higher up. Make you feel better?"

She shook her head. "Not really, but I don't have a choice, do I?"

"Not unless you want to skip the water. Feel free to try boiling it if you want. We might be able to find a rock somewhere around here."

She shooed him away. "Just go. I don't want to know any more."

He went, anticipating another interesting discussion over toilet paper, or lack thereof.

When he got back, he offered to help her dig a hole in the distance for taking care of her needs, but

she informed him she'd already taken care of things.
Not eager to have the discussion, he left it at that and
put several more logs by the fire. Then he sat beside
her in the small cave with his back to the rock wall,
wrapping the second blanket around his shoulders.

"What made you think I wanted a kid?"

She sounded genuinely confused, and he looked
over to find her practically scowling at the fire.

"Why else would an attractive woman like
yourself be looking for a one night stand?"

She looked over at him, her frown deeper. "So
women only want sex so they can get pregnant?
That's the stupidest thing I've ever heard. Are men
the only ones who can just have sex for fun? Or even
just relaxation?" She stumbled over the last bit, her
voice so quiet he barely heard it. Then he
remembered her comment about a prescription to fill.

He laughed. "No way. You were serious about
that whole prescription thing? Did your doctor
actually tell you to go have sex? That is awesome. I
really do want the name of that guy, just so I can go
shake his hand."

She stood up, clearly agitated. "Why do you even
care? We talked about this already. You don't want to
have sex with me, and for your information, I don't
want kids, now or ever. So why are we even talking
about this? It's ridiculous, and when I get back home
I'm going to tell Candace just that." She paced by the
fire, her hands punctuating each sentence sending

shadows scattering across the rocks. David considered stopping her, but sensed the most interesting part was yet to come, so he waited while she continued.

"I should have known asking her for advice was a bad idea. 'Don't be so uptight,' she said. 'Go on vacation, get laid, relax. Then you'll be able to sleep at night.' Yeah, right. I haven't slept a whole night since I left my house, and my nice, routine life. So far I've managed to make an idiot of myself several times, about got eaten by sharks, nearly drowned, and now I'm stranded on a damn deserted island. With the one guy on earth who doesn't want to sleep with me. If you'll excuse me, I think I'll just go throw myself in the ocean now."

David couldn't help it. He laughed, earning a rather mean glare as Kat stalked off into the dark trees. He waited for her to come back, but when she still hadn't reappeared a couple minutes later, he sighed and got to his feet. She'd gone in the direction of the stream rather than the beach, and he found her leaning against a tree on the bank, her shoulders shaking as she sobbed.

He stood just behind her, knowing she wouldn't welcome his touch just then.

"Your friend was right about one thing," he said, noting her muscles tense up at his voice. "You do need to relax, but you don't need a vacation or a fling to make that happen."

She shook her head. "Don't pretend you know me. You don't know anything about me."

He shrugged, unable to keep from reaching out and stroking her back with one hand. She flinched, but didn't pull away, and he noted how cold her skin was. She should have taken the blanket.

"I know you're feeling out of control right now. And I'm guessing you aren't a big 'go with the flow' type of person, right?"

She nodded, relaxing just a fraction under his touch. He stepped a little closer, giving her a little more of his heat.

"So maybe your friend thought getting away would help you let go a little easier. I take it that's not working?"

Kat nodded again, with a sniff. "I've been trying, but nothing works. I can't relax, I can't sleep, and I'm just...so tired..."

"I'll tell you what." David curled his hand around her waist and pulled her into his side. "Come back to the cave and warm up. Whether you sleep or not, at least you can get some rest. Did you know that studies have shown a twenty minute nap can sometimes be more restful than a full night's sleep? And our normal sleep cycles are an hour and a half each, on the average. So if you can sleep for either twenty minutes, or an hour and a half, you'll probably feel better."

"How do you know all that?" she asked, not resisting when he pulled her back toward the campsite. "I nap a lot."

He chuckled. "I hate mornings, and my boss was tired of me being late, and being groggy when I did manage to make it on time. She did the math and started telling me when I should go to bed to get up on time feeling decent. I don't always follow her suggestions, but I'll admit I do feel better when I do."

They reached the camp and he released her long enough to let her get settled just inside the cave, behind the fire. Picking up one of the warm blankets, he wrapped it around her and then sat beside her, using a small boulder as a backrest and wrapping himself up in the second blanket.

"Here," he said, reaching out to put his arm around her shoulders and pulled her toward him to lie on her side. She tensed, but didn't fight, and laid her head down on his leg as he stroked her arm with his fingers.

"Now just relax. Close your eyes, and rest. It doesn't matter if you sleep or not, just focus on the warm fire, the crackle of the flames, and how peaceful it is here."

Kat nodded, adjusting her head and shoulders until she seemed comfortable. David kept up a gentle, slow stroke as she settled in, letting his own body relax and soak in the heat as he felt her drifting off to sleep in his lap.

* * * *

Katherine woke to the now familiar sound of crackling flames and wondered how long she'd slept. Opening her eyes, she blinked and then frowned at the daylight surrounding the fire. She pushed up to a sitting position, glancing at the blanket that had been under her head. The last thing she remembered was David pulling her down to lay her head in his lap...

"Good morning. Sleep well?"

She looked across the fire at David as he stood staring down at her. Expecting a mocking smile at least, she was surprised and a little uncomfortable to see the genuine concern in his eyes.

"I think so, thanks to you. I...don't really know what to say, except to apologize for falling apart last night. Not one of my finer moments." She looked down at her hands, embarrassed.

"Don't worry about it," he said, moving closer to drop one of the imitation cardboard meal replacement bars in her lap. "I filled the canteen with fresh water too. When you're done, we'd better get moving. It's a decent size island, and we need to be on the other end by late afternoon to catch our ride back."

Grateful that he didn't want to make a big deal of it, Katherine washed down her breakfast with cool stream water, wishing for eggs and toast with juice instead. Getting up off the ground, she rolled up her blanket and put it in the emergency bag. Feeling vulnerable in just her bathing suit, she tied the lone towel around her waist and kicked dirt over the last few ashen embers.

"Ready to go Kat?" David reappeared from the direction of the stream, leaning down to take the bag from her hands before he walked off the way they'd come the night before. She hurried to catch up, torn between annoyance and curiosity.

"Why are we going back to the beach? I thought you said--"

He glanced over his shoulder at her. "We need to check on the boat, and see if there's a ship somewhere out looking for us past the reef. Then we can go, okay?"

His longer legs were eating up ground and Katherine had to practically jog to keep up. By the time they reached the sand, she was glad she'd taken all those spinning classes.

"Why can't we just take the boat around the island?" she asked. "Wouldn't that be faster? And we'd be able to take the boat back with us too. Or will we come get it when we get picked up?"

He shook his head. "I don't think there's enough gas to make it there. Amy and I can come back to get the boat another day - we run diving excursions over here all the time. It'll be okay here until then."

She followed him out onto the sand, already warm in the late morning sun. Holding a hand up to shield her face, she scanned the ocean, seeing nothing but waves and the dark outline of the reef in the distance.

"Is that a fin?" she asked, pointing to the water as they walked toward the boat. "It's awfully close to shore..."

He nodded. "There are some larger sharks that patrol the lagoon around here. Certain times of year are better than others, and they're normally quieter now, but with the weather changes lately their time tables could be changing. Did you say you nearly got eaten yesterday?"

She shrugged. "I may have been a bit dramatic, but there was a school or pack or whatever of smaller sharks following me for awhile. They were on top the reef though, so I figured they were those reef sharks you talked about."

He smiled as he checked the knots on the boat's anchor rope. "Not all sharks on the reef are reef sharks, but you didn't panic, and that's the important thing."

She frowned as he got a few more things out of the metal gear boxes.

"How do you know I didn't panic?"

Standing up, he grinned at her. "You didn't get eaten."

No arguing with that. "No, I didn't." She followed him as he ducked back into the forest, following his lead as they hiked through the trees.

"Why doesn't anyone live here?" she asked as they walked. It was a beautiful spot, so lush and green. Plenty of land and water too, it seemed. It would be the perfect place for a vacation hideaway, or one of those fancy resorts.

"Technically, this island is privately owned," he said, looking around as if someone might be listening. "I don't think the owner is here much, but I'm pretty sure if I owned a piece of paradise like this, I wouldn't want to sell or lease to anyone."

Katherine shivered. "I hope we don't get in trouble for trespassing. Are there even laws on a private island?"

"I'm not sure," David shrugged. "But I don't think we'll be here long enough to find out, so moot point."

As they continued the trek over the wild terrain, Katherine thought about what it would be like to own an island. She wasn't sure who could even afford to do that, much less how they would make enough money to buy an entire piece of land in the ocean. The idea of living in such complete isolation was both intriguing and terrifying.

And a little piece of her really wanted to experience it for herself. Only maybe not in the middle of the ocean.

David stopped suddenly at the top of a low rise and Katherine noticed too late. She ploughed into his back, making her struggle to keep from falling on her butt as he lurched forward with no choice but to jog down the slope that gave way to more sand on the other side. She stood at the top and watched as he skidded down the beach nearly to the tide line before he was finally able to stop.

"I'm sorry!" she called, going down more slowly to join him. "I was daydreaming, I guess. This place is so beautiful, but I can't imagine being stuck here for very long. I'd think it would get lonely."

"Depends on who you're stuck with." David wiggled his eyebrows and she knew she shouldn't laugh, but she couldn't quite hide a smile at the innuendo. As she looked over his shoulder, a bank of huge, angry looking clouds caught her eye. Her expression must have given her away as his own smile faded and he turned to look out to sea as well.

"Is that--"

He nodded. "Looks like a gnarly storm headed right for us. And it's coming from the direction of the main island too. We'd better get off the beach and find some shelter."

She started to follow as he jogged toward the trees, but then stopped.

"What about the boat? We'll miss our ride back!"

He shook his head and came back, grabbing her hand and pulling her along.

"The boat's not coming - Amy won't risk coming out in the middle of that squall. We'll have to try again tomorrow." He stopped at the edge of the jungle to look back briefly. "The storm is moving quickly - we don't have much time. Come on."

Katherine followed him as he ran back the way they'd come, doing her best to keep up as he jogged at an easy pace. Endurance training wasn't really her thing, and now she wished with all her heart she'd trained more.

As they raced over the dark damp earth, the sunlight glinted off of something to her right. Something big. She pulled out of David's grasp and stopped, breathing heavily as she squinted against the sun and peered through the trees.

"David, come here!" She waved for him, pointing excitedly at her discovery. "A house!"

He came back and bent down beside her, hands on his knees as he nodded.

"Probably the owner's place. It doesn't look all that sturdy though. We'd probably be better off against the rock face somewhere."

Katherine frowned, moving a step closer. "It looks pretty sturdy to me. Don't you think we should at least go check it out?"

He shook his head, grabbing her hand again. "You're just going to have to trust me on this, Kat. We need to find a cave or a cliff, and soon. There's no way to tell what that storm will bring, but I can't guarantee that house will be standing when it's over, so our best chance is to find the biggest rocks we can and shelter between them. We can come back and check out the house when the storm is gone."

"You can do what you want, but I'm going down there. And don't call me Kat, dammit!" She wrenched her hand out of his grasp and started toward the house. It was a house. Houses were solid. Houses were shelter. It was what they were meant to do, and the thought of being outside and exposed to the elements during a big storm was far more frightening than a house falling down over her.

A big gust of wind barreled through the valley and swooped through her path, nearly knocking her off her feet. When it was gone, David was there, standing in front of her with an apologetic look.

"I know you don't understand, and you're scared, but this could be life and death." Then he bent down and put his shoulder into her waist, wrapped his arms around her legs and slid her over his shoulder.

Shocked, Katherine hung there quietly for a moment as he carried her away from the house. She looked up to see it disappearing through the trees and couldn't stop the tears from falling as she pounded on his back.

"Let me down! Let me go right now! You can't do this!" She flailed her arms and tried to break loose, but his grip was like iron.

The wind howled relentlessly, covering her cries. Without any leverage her fists barely made contact as they went farther into the interior of the island. Realizing she was only wearing herself out, she settled, her heart pounding as the sky grew darker and the rain began to fall.

Chapter Four

Relieved to finally reach the base of the high rocky cliffs, David stopped to set Kat on her feet, making sure she hadn't passed out when she quieted down. She looked up at him, tired but resigned when he took her hand and tugged her forward in the rain. Moving along the face of the rock, he found a depression just barely big enough for the two of them sheltered by two huge boulders that must have fallen from the cliffs at some point. He tossed their bag into the depression and then scooted in after it, pulling her down to sit between his legs.

She shivered against him and he maneuvered a blanket from the bag to wrap around her, securing it with his arms. She turned toward the cliff with her face against his neck, and he barely heard the words she breathed across his skin.

"We're going to die, aren't we?"

Reaching up, he tucked a finger under her chin and forced her head back so he could look into her eyes.

"We are not going to die," he said, placing a gentle kiss on her lips, lingering a moment longer than he should have when she responded with the slightest movement of her mouth under his. "I promise."

He thought he felt a brief glimmer of hope spark between them in a lightening-lit moment before everything blacked out again. He held her tight, her head tucked under his chin as the storm raged on around them.

When the wind finally let up and the clouds cleared, it was moonlight that woke David from the light sleep he'd been falling in and out of for the duration.

"Is it over?" she asked, her voice groggy from sleep and misuse. He shifted, leaning out of their nest with one hand outstretched to feel for rain. Only a gentle breeze wafted over his skin.

"I think so," he said as she shifted her position, turning between his legs. "Careful getting up. The ground is still wet and probably slippery."

She braced one hand in his, grasping a depression in the rock with the other to pull herself up and out of the small cave. He watched her feet slide in the mud as she let go of his hand and moved to the side, barely keeping her balance.

"We should probably find a flat spot to spend the rest of the night," he said, hoisting himself carefully up beside her. "It's not safe to be walking around when the ground is so unstable." Glancing around, grateful that the moon was so bright, he spotted a large, flat rock sheltered by a circle of palm trees not too far away.

"Let's go over there." He pointed and then held out a hand as he began sloshing forward.

Kat's fingers closed around his and she took a tentative step away from the wall. Behind them, the ground sloped down which made forward motion tricky. They were nearly half-way to the rock when David felt Kat's arm jerk against his wrist. Then he was falling backward, landing heavily on the slick hill as Kat slipped away and gravity pulled him down after her.

Katherine flailed her arms to either side trying to find something to grab in the dark, her hands slippery and caked with thick mud. She turned to her stomach as gravity pulled her faster and faster down the slope, certain that when she finally stopped, it was going to hurt. A lot. Soon the ground beneath her fell away and she hung suspended for what seemed like several minutes before falling, falling, falling.

This was it then. When she hit the ground, it would all be over. She curled up into a ball, hugging her knees to her chest and praying that it wouldn't hurt for very long.

The impact jarred her body, sending a spray of water all around as she plummeted beneath. Disoriented, she broke her position and started to kick before realizing she wasn't sure which way was up. Forcing herself to still, she began to float, and kicked frantically in the direction her body wanted to go. As her head broke the water, she greedily gulped in air as she heard a second splash somewhere nearby.

"David?" She tried to swim towards the sound, the current fighting to drag her farther away. "David is that you?"

Something brushed her leg. Pulled. Her head dipped underwater and she panicked, kicking and flailing to reach the surface again. Fighting to keep her head above water, she felt fingers wrap around her wrist and the pressure on her ankle eased.

"It's me, Kat." David's voice came from beside her in the darkness, and she breathed a sigh of relief even as she struggled to tread water with just one arm. "I just don't want us to get separated again. Can you float?"

She nodded, and then realized he couldn't see her any more than she could see him. Down here in the valley, the moon was completely blocked by the trees.

"Yes."

"Good. Lay on your back, feet towards me so the current is pushing us feet first. I'll try to get us headed toward one of the banks."

Katherine did as he asked, using her free arm to help him steer them toward the left side of the river. The sheer force of the current was shocking, considering it had been a gentle roll when they'd broke camp.

David's grip tightened and he felt more...solid, somehow. That's when she realized they were no longer moving.

"You should be able to stand here," he said, helping her as she lowered her feet and caught her balance in the waist-high water. The air was cold as she stood up, and she began to shiver uncontrollably as she waded behind him up onto a small rocky beach. The roar of the ocean was close, and she frowned, turning her head this way and that in an attempt to figure out where it was in relation to them.

"We need to build a fire, and quick," he said, leading her farther up the rocky ground. "Unfortunately, I didn't think to grab the bag out of our little cave up there, so no matches. Not that it would matter, I guess - I would have lost it in the fall."

Katherine crossed her arms over her chest, attempting to stop the now-constant tremors that wracked her body.

"Ho c-c-can w-w-we?" she managed to push out through her uncooperative lips. She felt a hand tentatively brush her arm and instinctively moved toward it. His arm curled around her, drawing her close and encircling her body with the other arm.

"We'll figure it out." He was cold too, his skin like ice as she leaned against him and laid her head against his shoulder. "I'm not sure where we're going to find any kind of dry wood to use for the fire - everything is drenched and I can't see a damn thing. But we might be able to spark something up with a couple of rocks."

He pulled back and her whole body shivered at the loss of contact. She wasn't sure she could even pick up a rock, much less strike two together. Her teeth chattered and she yawned as she tried to think of some other way to warm up.

The only thing she could think of after being in David's arms did make her blush, though he'd already turned her down. That didn't mean they couldn't share body heat though...

"We're c-c-close to the b-b-beach, right? I mean the sand, not this rocky stuff..."

"I think so." She could just barely make his silhouette out as he moved closer again. "Got an idea?"

She shrugged. "What if we just dug out a pit for ourselves and huddled together under a layer of sand? The digging would help us warm up, and body heat could do the rest." She paused, waiting for a response. When he remained silent, she wished she'd kept quiet.

"Stupid, I know. If you want to go look for something to burn, I can try to knock some of these rocks toge--"

"That is a very good idea," David said, reaching out to grab her hand. "We might even find some residual heat if we dig in the right spot. If you feel a big stick or something we can dig with while we're walking, let me know. I'm pretty sure the beach is this way." He tugged her hand and she followed, once again glad for the thin rubber covering her feet.

She couldn't possibly reply to the big stick comment in her present frame of mind. She wasn't sure what had gotten into her as she smiled at the mental image he'd given her. Snuggled on his lap in the cave had given her a pretty good idea of just how big his personal stick was, the thought making her lick her lips. Warmth sparked somewhere inside as she walked with him, doing her level best to banish the naughty thoughts from her head.

Obviously something was very wrong with her. No woman in her right mind would be thinking about sex at a time like this. Still, she couldn't think of a better way to generate some of that body heat they needed.

Damn Murphy's Law for stranding her on a deserted island with a guy who wasn't even remotely interested. Though there had been that kiss...

"Found one!" David held something long and round up, and Katherine realized she wasn't imagining it, she could actually see more than just a shadow-shape. Tilting her head back, she looked up to see a dim yellow-white glow illuminating thick clouds above.

"Nice job," she said, turning her attention back to David and just barely suppressing the urge to snicker at his big stick. "We should find the beach while we have a little light - who knows if those clouds are going to move for good or not."

He turned a slow circle, taking in their surroundings. "I think we need to go that way." He used the stick to point forward and to the right. "It feels like the storm is over though - and it's definitely getting warmer, so I bet those clouds will float away quicker than you might think."

Katherine followed him as he set off through the trees. Now that he mentioned it, it did actually feel warmer, though she thought maybe it was because they were moving around.

Or it could be because you're a total perv.

Mentally rolling her eyes at herself, she shook her head, looking up just in time to see David stopped in front of her, his expression curious.

Busted!

"What?" she said, giving him as stern of a frown as she could muster. No easy feat given she actually hadn't felt so relaxed in years. Maybe she had hypothermia, or was just going crazy? That had to be it. No other explanation.

"You were just smiling." His lips turned up in a slow, seductive grin she suspected he'd practiced on many, many women. "What's going on in that head of yours? Why so happy all of a sudden?"

"I am not happy," Kat said, giving him a stern look so obviously fake that it reminded him of a sexy lawyer getting ready to bust out of her gray suit and white button down shirt. Too bad she didn't have a pair of those black rimmed glasses. He was pretty sure that would be the end of him.

Stepping closer, he brandished the long branch he'd found. "Were you laughing at my big stick? Because most women would appreciate that, you know."

The corners of her mouth crooked up and she looked away as he took another step into her personal space.

"Of course not." Her voice was a little strangled, and she took a deep breath, exhaling before she looked at him again. "This is a life or death situation. That would be completely inappropriate."

He shrugged, closing the last bit of distance between them and sliding his free hand around her waist. "It doesn't really seem like either of us is in immediate danger of dying, though we really should get warmed up. It would be tragically ironic to die of hypothermia on a deserted tropical island."

Kat laughed, a quiet, nervous sound as the movement pressed her curves tighter against his body.

"Yes it would," she answered, tentatively putting her trembling hands on his chest. "That's why I suggested we share body heat. In the sand. Sand is a good conductor of heat."

He nodded, dropping the stick so he could put his other arm around her. "You know what creates heat, right?"

She tilted her head, thinking for a minute. "Fire? But we already decided--"

"Friction."

Her eyes grew wide as the word hung suspended between them.

"Like this?" she whispered, rubbing her hands lightly up and down over his chest.

He slid his hands down to the small of her back, his fingers pressing her hips tight against his pelvis.

"Like this." He bent down to capture her lips, licking and nibbling until she opened to him, her hands creeping up to caress the back of his neck.

She whimpered just a little as he deepened the kiss, her tongue darting out to tease him as he devoured her mouth. His cock hardened between them, wanting - needing release, and he bent his knees just enough to hoist Kat up as she wrapped those long legs around his waist.

Her core centered right where he wanted it, David eyeballed the nearest tree and sandwiched her between his body and the trunk, slipping one hand from her back to caress a firm breast. Her head tilted back and he placed a line of nipping kisses down her neck as his thumb flicked the tight nipple straining at the fabric of her swimsuit. She moaned louder this time, her back arching as she ground her center against his erection, nearly driving him mad with need as her moisture seeped through his shorts.

Shifting slightly, he reached between them and freed himself, then slipped a finger under the elastic of the damp fabric between her legs and pulled it to the side. As he slid inside her tight sheath, she sighed, sinking down over him like a silk glove. A perfect fit.

Stilling for the moment, she raised her head to look at him, her eyes half-mast in the moonlight and foggy with lust. He flexed his hips, pulsing deep within her and she gasped, tightening around him.

It was the sweetest sound he'd ever heard.

He kissed her again, thrusting slowly, deeply as he swallowed each tiny whimper. She felt...exquisite locked around him, her feet urging him on as he moved between her legs.

"Faster," she whispered between kisses, leaning back against the tree and pulling the suit straps off her shoulders to reveal those sweet, succulent breasts. She grasped the branch overhead with both hands, thrusting her pert nipples toward him as her inner muscles pulled him in tighter. "Harder. Please. I need more."

He chuckled, transfixed by the sight of her hanging there impaled on his cock, displayed for his pleasure.

He never should have said no that first night.

Grasping her hips, he pulled out nearly all the way, and then without warning, slammed himself home.

"Like that, Kitty-Kat?" he asked, pulling back again and expecting a harsh retort. Instead, she nodded, squeezing his cock tight again.

"Oh yeah," she breathed, her hips moving forward to meet him as he slammed deep into her core again. "Yessss," she hissed. "Just like that. More!"

Her head fell back and he gave her what she wanted, his hips pistoning in and out as he fucked her hard against the tree.

Katherine felt like her entire body was about to explode as David thrust deep and didn't withdraw, holding her hips immobile as he ground his pelvis in small circles. The motion hit all her sensitive spots both inside and out, and she couldn't hold off any longer.

She cried out as her body contracted, her inner muscles spasming around him as she jerked within his hold. Deep within she felt his release, hot fluid mingling with hers, flooding her with his essence as her legs remained locked around his waist. For a few moments, her entire world was light and heat and pure, unadulterated bliss.

Then she shivered as a cool draft blew over her bare breasts, bringing her back to the reality of her situation.

"Let go - I've got you."

David's voice was low and gruff as he stepped closer and wrapped his arms around her back, pressing a light kiss between her breasts. Releasing her hold on the branch overhead she grasped his neck, her legs trembling as she forced herself to loosen her grip so he could put her down.

Empty. She couldn't describe the feeling any other way as he left her braced against the tree so he could pull up his shorts and fasten them. Suddenly she remembered why she didn't have sex. Why one night stands were a really bad idea. While they lasted, it was the most awesome thing on the planet.

But that empty feeling afterward when it was time to say goodbye? It never really went away.

Forcing herself to move, she adjusted her suit, putting everything back in the right places to cover herself as much as possible. David moved closer, pulling her into his embrace and she went willingly, thankful she didn't have to look at him just yet.

"Warmer?" he murmured, idly caressing her back. She nodded against his chest.

"You were right," she said, forcing herself to smile to hide the sadness. "Friction does create heat."

He chuckled, the sound vibrating his chest against her cheek until he pulled back to look down at her. Lifting her head to meet his gaze in the dim light of early dawn, she was surprised at the range of emotions reflected back at her. Was it possible he felt more than just a passing attraction?

His smile faded and he bent to kiss her once, gently. For a moment she thought he might say something...profound. Something to reassure her that what they'd shared wasn't all there was. But as the silence stretched between them and he stepped away with a quick rub of his hands on her arms, she knew in the pit of her stomach that it wasn't going to happen.

"It's starting to get light," he said, his back to her. "I think the beach is that way. We should see if we can find something to eat, and then we'll wait for the boat." He half-turned back to glance at her. "Is that okay with you?"

She nodded, blinking to hold back the tears. "Of course," she replied, her voice surprisingly steady. "Lead the way."

Chapter Five

David led the way through the trees, feeling like a world-class jerk. He knew Kat was looking for a sign that what they'd done had meant something, but he couldn't mislead her like that. Being with her had been better than he ever could have imagined, and they definitely had a real connection, but realistically that's as far as it could go.

He glanced behind him, making sure she still followed. Her head was bent down, her eyes focused on the ground as she moved carefully through the scattered branches and rocks. Her shoulders were slumped and she looked exhausted, clearly pushing herself to keep up. The sky was growing lighter by the minute, and he could see the cut lines of her muscles as she moved, a beautifully graceful sight.

She stopped, looking up at him with a curious expression.

"Is something wrong?" she asked.

He shook his head. "Everything's fine. You holding up okay?"

Kat nodded, giving him a small smile. "I'm tired, but I'll be okay. Not to sound like a five-year old, but do you think we're getting closer?"

"Absolutely." He pointed to his left. "The cabin we saw should be just over there. We'll stop there and see if anyone's home. I didn't see a boat, but maybe it's in a smaller cove somewhere. We'll ask."

"Well let's go then," she said, moving closer. "Anything that will get me back to civilization and a hot shower is just fine with me."

David chuckled as she caught up. "Come on then. Not too much further."

She walked beside him as they zigzagged down a gentle slope and out onto a rocky beach. Just as he'd thought, the cabin - or what was left of it - sat on tall stilts overlooking the water. The back of the structure stood strong, but the front and sides were torn apart, wood and plaster hanging loose and gaping holes in the roof. Kat stopped to survey the damage.

"This is why you wouldn't let me come down here last night." Tilting her head, she looked thoughtfully at him. "Thank you."

He gave her a slight nod in acknowledgment. "Let's see if there's anything salvageable inside. It seems unlikely since I'm sure this isn't the first storm to hit the place, but we've got a little time to poke around."

When they reached the stilts, David threw his weight against each in turn, checking for any signs of instability. None of them moved or swayed though, and he decided it was safe enough to go up. They found a ladder made of thick branches and rope secured to one of the back posts, and used that to climb up and under the wrap-around railing.

"Maybe you should wait below," David said as he stepped off the ladder. The platform was tilted slightly, with holes every few feet. Kat climbed up beside him and shook her head.

"No way. You don't get to have all the fun." She moved toward a beaten down wall half-standing and mostly torn to shreds, stopping at an empty window frame to peer inside.

"Be careful where you step," David warned as Kat stepped over the sill into what appeared to be the main living quarters. "Any of this wood could be rotten - you'd fall right through."

"I will."

He watched Kat gingerly poke the floor beams with a toe before taking each step as she moved toward a big steamer trunk against the back wall. He followed, looking around the space for anything that looked remotely usable. Most of the furniture was still there, bolted to the floor with the upholstery long gone. He wondered how long the place had been abandoned.

"Ha!" Kat cried, and he turned her way to see her holding up several items of clothing. "They were in the trunk...and still dry!" She pulled a long-sleeved shirt over her head, the arms dangling well past her fingers. Fumbling with the extra fabric, she wiggled her way into a pair of light pants and tied the drawstring waist to hold them up. Rolling her sleeves, she left them on her forearm and then turned around, arms outstretched.

"Like it?" she asked, smiling.

He shrugged. "It's okay. Seems like a pity to cover all that lovely skin of yours up though."

She laughed. "Sorry, but I'm tired of running around in nothing but a swimsuit, so you're going to have to live. There's more - did you want dry things?"

He thought about it and then declined. "I think I'll pass. My clothes are dry, and the sun's coming up so I'll be okay. Are you ready to go? We should find some food."

"Sure." Kat carefully retraced her steps to join him, and then shimmied down the ladder, waiting for him at the bottom. "Without fire we can't really cook a fish and we lost our emergency supplies. What else is there?"

David smiled, pointing up at a nearby stand of coconut trees. "Everything you could want in one seed," he said, jogging over to where several large brown globes lay on the ground. Holding one up, he held it out to her and then picked out one for himself.

"Breaking them open is the tricky part, but we can drink the liquid inside and then eat the meat. Good for you, and tasty too. Let me show you."

* * * *

The coconut wasn't exactly her thing, but Katherine had to admit it did perk her up. She munched on a chunk of the milky white meat as they continued the trek to the end of the island. The sun rose high and hot, and by the time she could see the tide sliding up over sand she was sweating in her newly found clothing.

David stopped just short of the warming sand and pointed to a sandbar out in the sea.

"Amy should be able to pick us up on that sandbar," he said, shielding his face with one hand as he scanned the horizon. "We can walk out over there when the tide goes down a little more. We'll just have to be careful not to get stuck - it's a long swim back if she doesn't make it."

Katherine scrunched up her nose, not keen on that idea at all.

"We should have brought the boat. Remind me why we didn't just hop in and motor around the island?"

"Not enough gas," he said, stepping onto the sand. "So walking was pretty much our only option."

"Right." She followed him, her feet sinking past the sun-warmed top layer of fine grit through to the cooler layers below. "So we're just going to wade out to the middle of the sandbar and wait to be stranded there when the tide goes out? There has to be a better plan than that..."

He chuckled, sounding far more annoyed than amused. "I'm all ears, Kat. If you have a better suggestion, don't be shy."

"Katherine. And I think we should make a signal or something to let her know where we are. Then if she comes, we can wade out there, and if she doesn't, we're stuck on the beach instead of surrounded by water and sharks again. I've had enough sharks for awhile, if it's all the same to you."

"What kind of signal did you have in mind? I think we can safely rule out a fire, and it seems like that's the only thing that would be visible from way out there. What else you got? And why do you mind me calling you Kat so much?"

She sighed. "I don't know. I just really don't think we should get stuck out there. And my name is Katherine, not Kat. That should be reason enough."

"Try again, sweetheart." He moved closer, running a finger just inside the vee of her shirt. "Kat is a perfectly good nickname, and honestly, you're very cat-like, so it suits you. I want to know why you don't like it."

"It wasn't a compliment in grade school. I hated it then, and I hate it now. Just let it go, okay?"

David knew he should let it drop, but he couldn't seem to keep from prodding her.

"No." He moved closer yet, his fingers moving down between her breasts to span across her ribcage. "The problem is, when I hear Katherine, I think of a quiet librarian who hides away in dark stacks and needs to be coaxed out of her shell. There's nothing wrong with that, and I get that you want the world to think you're that person, but hard as you try, you're just not her."

She tried to protest, but he brought his other hand up between them, laying three fingers over her mouth.

"No, you're feisty, and sexy, and everything about you makes people sit up and take notice. You project confidence and even when the claws come out, you're still too cute to be mad at for long..."

Kat tried to step back, but he held her in place, raising his eyebrows. "Going somewhere?"

"Let me go, or I'll use these too-cute claws on the side of your face." Her words were almost a growl which just made him smile more.

"See, that right there is what I mean. You are gorgeous when you're angry, and extremely sensual when you're not." He stroked his hand up and down her back, slowly, smoothly.

"Just relax, Kat. Let me pet you a little. Better yet, you can curl up in my la--ouch!"

He released her quickly as the flat of her hand connected solidly with his jaw. Reaching up to feel the burning in his face, he wasn't prepared when she threw herself at him from the side, tackling him to the ground and straddling his hips while she pinned his arms overhead.

"I'm not a mousey librarian," she said, her pulse beating rapidly against the skin of his wrists through her fingers. "But I'm not a social butterfly willing to just sleep with anyone either, which is what the name Kat means to a lot of people. I don't want to be that woman - can you understand that?"

David figured it wasn't a good time to remind her she'd come to the big island with the express purpose of getting laid. Instead, he slowly nodded his head.

"I understand wanting to redefine yourself," he said carefully. "But can't you be both Katherine and Kat? Different sides of yourself, but both still 'you'?"

She thought for a moment, her gaze wandering somewhere past his head. Then she sat back, narrowly missing the family jewels, and released his wrists.

"Kat scares me," she finally said, so softly he almost missed it. She ran her hands through her hair and looked up at the sky, the backs of her thighs resting on the front of his. If she'd just scoot up a few inches...

He reached out to grasp her hands, moving her forward to where he wanted her. Bending his legs, he created a back rest for her and then released her hands.

"What scares you the most about her?"

She gave a little half-laugh. "Everything." She glanced down at him, her defenses lowered long enough for him to see the abject fear in her eyes before she looked away again.

"You don't know what I'm like - not really. I like schedules and routines and everything in its place. I hate change. I get antsy every time I have to make an unplanned change to my day. It was nerve-wracking just getting on the plane to come here without any plans or itinerary other than the return flight. And then you...and this screwed up trip..." she rubbed her face with one hand. "I just need to go home, and get back into my normal routine. Everything will be fine if I can just do that."

"Run and hide, you mean?" David said, propping one arm under his head so he could look up at her. "Because that's what you'll be doing. It won't actually fix anything. You'll be stuck where you always were. And wasn't that the reason for coming here - to learn how to meld both worlds together?"

There was truth to his words that Katherine didn't want to face. She was trying to decide how to answer when a small but unmistakable shape floated into her vision out in the open sea.

"Run," she said, getting hastily to her feet. "We both need to run. Now!"

Reaching for his hand to pull him to his feet, she couldn't make her mouth move fast enough and simply pointed to answer his confused and irritated look.

"Boat! Ship! Whatever - we have to catch it!"

He didn't need any further explanation, taking off in the direction of the exposed sandbar. She followed as closely as she could, minding the odd bits of rock and driftwood sticking up on the beach. The surface of the sandbar wasn't really all that sandy, but rather hard and jagged, and she had trouble keeping her balance. Somehow she did though, almost catching up as they reached a point in front of the passing ship.

"Is that your boat?" she asked, bent over with her hands on her knees as she tried to catch her breath. He shielded his eyes and squinted against the glare off the water.

"I can't tell. Doesn't matter though. Looks like they saw us. See the dingy being lowered?"

Katherine nodded. "Oh thank God. I don't think I've ever wanted a warm shower and a soft bed more than I do right now."

David chuckled. He glanced sideways at her, then returned his gaze to the small boat making its way to them.

"You didn't answer my question. And I still want to know the answer," he said, just loud enough to be heard over the waves.

Katherine shrugged, looking down at the crevices and lines of the sandbar beneath her feet. "I came to relax. So I could sleep. So far I've done very little relaxing, and more sleeping that I could have hoped for, so I suppose it was a success. But this isn't real life, David. I can't function like this. So melding those two personalities into something I can live with is something I'll need to work on at home. I don't know how else to do it."

He nodded as the boat drew closer. "Sounds like a solid plan." He waved at the woman in the boat, and Katherine realized with relief that it was Amy, the Captain from the day before.

"Thought you might be waiting," she called out as she got the small craft as close to the sandbar as possible. "Sorry I couldn't get back last night - that was a hell of a storm."

"No problem," David said, gesturing for Katherine to board first. "We did okay, all things considered. But we'll be glad to get back to the main island."

Katherine stood at the edge of the sandbar and reached for the side of the boat, but it was too far away.

"You're gonna have to get wet," Amy said. "Come on, I'll help you up."

Nodding, Katherine took a breath and stepped into the ocean, bobbing quickly to the surface with a gasp at the temperature drop. Swimming the few feet out, she reached up and grasped the edge of the boat, pulling her legs up sideways as Amy helped anchor her arms by the wrist. As soon as she was settled, David was climbing in beside her. Wrapped up in a thick towel, a strong sense of exhaustion came over Katherine as she listened to David and Amy banter on the way back to the ship.

Chapter Six

When they reached the ship, David helped Kat climb aboard and then left her to get settled while he helped Amy secure the dingy and prepare to head back to the main island. When he finally thought to look for Kat again, he found her stretched out on the same padded bench she'd ridden out on, fast asleep. He covered her with a blanket and then went to the control room.

"So did you shag her?" Amy asked with a wry smile. "She looks slightly less tense than she did yesterday, which is odd considering what I imagine you've been through."

David shrugged. Normally he was eager to share his conquest stories, especially since he knew it drove Amy mad. But this time, he wasn't sure. With Kat it had been...different.

Could he afford to let it be?

"You better believe it," he said, forcing the usual cockiness into his voice. "What woman could possibly keep her hands off this body while stranded on a deserted island? You excepted, of course." He laughed, but it sounded too loud even to his own ears. Amy shot him a knowing look, her lips tugged up in a told-you-so smirk.

"I do believe you might be falling for this one, David. The only question now is, are you man enough to see it through? Or will you send her off like all the others with a quick kiss and a promise to call that you never intend to keep?"

He clutched dramatically at his heart, stumbling back at her words.

"Ow! You should be careful with those barbs. You could put an eye out or something."

Amy shook her head. "You're seriously going to do it, aren't you? Just let her go because you're more afraid to let her in than to lose her. I'm disappointed, but not surprised."

"Nah," David scoffed, "it's not like that anyways. She was only looking for a quick lay so she could sleep, and I gave it to her. Now she can go home to what sounds like a pretty boring life, and I can go back to harassing island girls. Win-win."

He happened to glance toward the door and felt his heart drop into his stomach at the expression on Kat's face. Hurt and dismay followed quickly by that mask of cold indifference he'd seen too many times before. He tried to remember why it had been so important to hide his true feelings from Amy, but couldn't think of a single good reason in that instant.

It didn't matter now though, judging by the ice in Kat's eyes. He'd just lost her.

At the sudden silence, Amy turned to look at him, and then followed his gaze to Kat. "Oh wow. I'm...we didn't know you were there. Is there something you need?"

Kat gave the Captain a wan smile. "I was just wondering if you had any bottled water. I woke up kind of thirsty. It's okay if you don't - I'd hate to be a bother."

Amy scowled at David. "You're not a bother, and there's water in the cooler to your right. Help yourself to anything you want."

"Thank you." Kat walked away without another word.

"You are such an idiot," Amy said, turning back to watch as they sailed closer to the docks. David stepped closer and lowered his voice.

"You didn't even like her yesterday, so what do you care? Besides, you're the one who started it."

She shook her head. "Whatever. I need to dock this thing, and you need to go talk to her, since we both know you were lying through your damn teeth and she's obviously not just messing around. Get out of the cockpit. That's an order."

Katherine quickly blinked back the tears as she saw David approach out of the corner of her eye. She picked up the towels she'd used and tossed them in a hamper, then gathered her things while he watched.

"I'm sorry," he said, keeping his distance. "You know how guys are. They always say stupid stuff to their buddies about girls. It's just a thing we do. And Amy's more like a guy friend, you know?"

Katherine forced herself to look up at him and smile.

"Nothing to be sorry about," she said, taking care to use a chipper tone. "Everything you said was the truth. I wanted to get laid so I could sleep. Mission accomplished, and I appreciate you helping me out." The boat bumped against the dock and she saw David look at the moorings, and then back at her.

"Are you going to secure the boat? I'd better start checking on things like my hotel room and a flight home. I just hope the airline will understand and change my ticket. Flying is just so expensive, don't you think?" She knew she was rambling, but couldn't seem to help it. He knew too, judging by the look he was giving her, but he said nothing.

He finally nodded and turned away, jumping down onto the dock to tie the ropes to the moorings. Just as well.

She put her bag over her shoulder and waved to Amy as she opened the gate in the railing and hopped down to the wooden deck below. Stifling the urge for one more glance over her shoulder, she walked up the dock to the beach and headed for the hotel.

The next few hours were a nightmare.

Her little beach hut had been cleaned out and given to someone else, so she had to pay for a small room within the hotel proper, all they had available on short notice. At least they still had her suitcase and clothes. She'd write David's scuba tours company for a refund later.

After a shower and a change of clothes, she called the airline only to be told that her non-refundable return ticket couldn't be transferred, and that she'd have to book another flight home at full price. It took some wrangling, but she was finally able to reserve a seat the next afternoon, maxing out her credit card.

Head hurting and beaten down, she lay on the bed and tried to sleep. Tossing and turning, she finally gave in to the tears simmering just below the surface. How had everything gotten so messed up?

Half an hour later, she got up and washed her face, looking at herself in the mirror. The woman staring back at her was foreign with tanned skin and loose, tousled hair. Very different from her normal put-together professional self. The dark circles she recognized, but that haunted, lost look in her eyes was another new, unwelcome change.

David had done that. Or rather, she'd let him, which was worse. Candace was wrong. Opening herself up had just made it worse, and for what? A couple nights of sleep? Memories that would take too long to fade?

With a heavy sigh, she turned away and grabbed the last of her cash and key card. No sense in wasting the night sitting alone with her depressing thoughts. She'd find something to eat, and then watch the sun go down on the beach. A fitting end to a disastrous vacation.

Especially if it involved a Mai Tai. Or two.

* * * *

The sun was just beginning to set as David walked up the beach. He'd tried to stay away, but he needed to see Kat once more before she left. Needed to apologize again for...everything. Having just interrupted what appeared to be an intimate moment involving whipped cream and chocolate syrup at what used to be her hut, he was on his way to the hotel in hopes she hadn't found a flight out yet.

Glancing to the right, he saw the dark profile of a beautiful woman in the distance. Sitting in the sand, she held a hurricane glass in one hand while the other wrapped around one knee. Her hair drifted gently around her shoulders with the breeze, and though he couldn't see her features, he knew her.

Switching course, he went to her side. Lowering himself to the sand, he sat beside her and watched quietly as the huge orange ball slid down under the horizon. The fact that she let him was encouraging, he supposed.

When the last vestiges of light were gone, she finally spoke.

"I fly out tomorrow afternoon."

"Okay." His stomach flipped over, his chest tightened. There were so many things to be said, and he didn't know how to say any of them. Didn't even know where to start. But it couldn't end, not yet. Not like this.

"Kat, I--"

A gentle touch on his arm stilled him, drew his gaze up. He could just make out the haunted look in her eyes, the sad smile on her lips. She got to her feet, holding a hand out to him.

"Shhh. Let's just go."

He took her hand and she helped him up, lacing her fingers with his as they walked up the beach to the hotel. She led him down a long hall in the older part of the building and into a small room with a double bed and not much else. After she locked the door, she turned and leaned against the door as he watched.

"I know I'm just another island fling," she said, holding a hand up when he would have protested. "It's okay. I get it. And you can say no if you want to. But I was hoping..."

She pushed off the door and moved in close, sliding her hands up over his shoulders to play with the hair at the back of his neck.

"I was hoping you would stay. Just for tonight."

He grasped her hips, pulling her tight against his body and wrapping his arms around her. His lips found hers, teasing.

"So you can sleep?" he murmured against her delectable lips. He wasn't sure why it mattered, but it did.

She moaned low in her throat as he kissed her, slow and gentle.

"No," she breathed when he finally let her up for air. "Because I want you."

He captured her mouth again, feasting on her as he spun her around. Her hands worked between them, undoing buttons and zippers and pulling off his clothes and he happily returned the favor. Finally down to skin-on-skin they ended up on the bed, somehow. He settled between her legs, the tip of his cock probing gently at the entrance between her thighs, but no further. Not yet.

He worshiped her neck with his lips, traced her collarbone with his tongue, laved and suckled at her nipples while she arched off the bed into his mouth, her soft whimpers driving him crazy with need. Kissing and caressing he worked his way down her body, across her ribs and over her stomach, laved at her navel as it undulated under his touch.

So soft. So beautiful. So irresistible.

Opening her inner lips with his fingers, he caught her clitoris between his lips, flicking the sensitive bud with his tongue as her hips rolled up, begging for more. Swirling in circles he drove her to the edge before moving lower still, lapping hungrily at the warm juices flowing from her core.

"David, please," she panted, her thighs clamped around his head as he thumbed her clit. "I need you inside me. Now."

Her legs fell open and he crawled up her body, sealing his lips over hers as he thrust inside her waiting warmth.

His balls tightened as he moved within her, knowing he should slow down, but needing to claim her. To leave his mark. Bracing himself on his elbows, he looked down, watching her beautiful face as the pressure built between them.

"Open your eyes," he said, gyrating his hips in a small circle and earning a surprised gasp. Her lashes fluttered up and she met his stare, showing him a wealth of emotion in those shimmering depths.

He slowed his movements, lazily sliding in and out as he brushed the hair back from her face.

"Don't leave," he said, burying himself deep within her and holding there. "Stay with me. Be my one and only island girl."

She hesitated and then looked away, closing her eyes as the tears spilled over. Shutting him out.

"I can't. I'm sorry."

Her inner muscles clenched around his cock, pulling him in tighter even as disappointment and loss flooded through his very being. Her ankles locked around his waist and he leaned down to place gentle kisses along her neck. Slowly he began to move again, savoring the feel of her surrounding him, knowing it would truly be the last time. She urged him on with her legs, faster, deeper, and he gave her what she wanted as the tension between them twisted and grew until he couldn't hold back any longer.

She cried out, her back arching off the bed as she met his last hard thrusts, the sight of her making his own release that much stronger. He collapsed on top of her and rolled to the side, his head in the crook of her neck as he focused on catching his next breath.

Kat rolled toward him, moving down to snuggle her face against his chest as he pulled a blanket up over them and held her tight. Less than five minutes later, her breathing evened out and he smiled, kissing her forehead before he drifted off to sleep.

When he woke, warm sunlight was streaming in through the sheer curtains. Memories from the night before came back in a rush, and he reached for Kat, his body craving hers. But the other side of the bed was empty, and even as he sat up to look for her, he knew she was already gone.

Chapter Seven

"You look like hell. I hate to admit this, but I may have been wrong to send you on a vacation."

Katherine stepped out of her friend's hug and gave her a wry smile as they started toward the baggage claim. She'd called Candace from the airport that morning to let her know which flight she'd be on, and now she kind of wished she'd just grabbed a cab instead.

Except she had no cash left.

"It's been a rough week." An understatement if there ever was one. It was all kind of surreal though, now that she was back in familiar surroundings. Like an odd dream.

An odd dream with a hot guy and mind-blowing sex.

She felt her cheeks heating up, and knew she needed to get that under control before Candace noticed.

"How about you? How was your week? Same old, same old?" She glanced over, surprised to see a blush spreading across the other woman's cheeks. She grinned, relieved to have something besides her own problems to think about for once.

"Something did happen! Tell Dr. Katherine. Is it a guy?"

Candace shrugged. "You could say that, I guess. I...sort of have a houseguest now. A very tall, comfortable-in-a-towel houseguest. It's disconcerting, to be honest."

"Ooo-la-la!" Katherine laughed, grabbing her bag off the conveyer as it slid by. "It's about time you took your own advice. When do I get to meet him?"

Candace shook her head and held up both hands, her eyes wide. "No way. He's not staying. I mean, we're not together. It's temporary, and purely platonic. No need for introductions." She dropped her hands and motioned for Katherine to follow. "Now come on. I'm taking you home, and you're going to tell me all about your trip."

It wasn't far to her house, and it felt weird walking into her tidy, organized home after a week of chaos and minute-to-minute living. Dropping her bag on the floor, she set her keys on the table and kicked off her shoes, leaving them in the hall as she padded across the living room to the kitchen in stocking feet. By the time Candace leaned against the kitchen doorframe, she was setting up the coffee pot.

"Caff or decaf?" Katherine asked, waiting with one hand on the cupboard door. Candace tilted her head, looking at her like Katherine imagined she looked at lab rats. Or would, if she worked in a lab.

"Caff is fine." She watched intently as Katherine filled the filter and started the machine, taking two cups down and setting them side by side on the counter. Finally, Katherine looked up.

"What? Why are you staring at me like that?"

Candace raised her eyebrows and glanced back over her shoulder pointedly before walking over to the table and sitting down.

"You do realize that before you left, you never would have left your shoes and bag in the hall, right? Your keys would have been hung up, and you would have had to unpack before we could sit down." She paused, and Katherine looked at her feet, waiting for the need to go unpack to wash over her. But it never came.

It could wait.

"Was I really that bad?" She switched the coffee pot for a cup, and then held the other one under the stream, replacing the pot before carrying both cups to the table.

Candace gave a noncommittal shrug. "Bad is a relative term. I like different better. You've changed, Katherine. Tell me what happened."

"Everything?" Katherine practically held her breath, not wanting to say a word and yet barely able to contain the pressure that had been building ever since she'd left David in bed that morning.

Candace smiled, settling back into her chair. "Everything."

Two hours, a relocation to the living room and three cups of coffee later, Candace set her cup on the end table next to the couch and leaned forward.

"So you just left him there, sleeping? No goodbye, no note, not even an email address?"

Katherine shook her head, curling her legs up in the big armchair. "What's the point? His life is there, mine is here. He doesn't want to settle down - he said as much. So why stay in contact? It would only be prolonging the inevitable."

Candace's cell phone rang for the third time in half an hour. She looked at the display and sighed.

"A client?"

"No." Candace rubbed a hand over the side of her face. "It's Emmett. That house guest I told you about. I have no idea what he could possibly want. He's been here long enough that he knows where everything is."

Katherine grinned. "Maybe he's lonely. He just wants to talk to you. Why don't you just go home and see what he needs? You've heard my sordid tale, and I'm wiped out, honestly. We can chat more later, and you can tell me all about this guy." She wiggled her eyebrows, earning an eye roll in return.

As if on cue, the phone rang again. Candace sighed, and answered the call.

"What do you need?"

Katherine could just hear a man's voice on the other end.

"Candy! About time you picked up. There's a guy here who says he's your boyfriend. Won't leave until he sees you, and he seems to want to pummel me into the ground. I need you here, like an hour ago. Where are you?"

Candace closed her eyes. "I told you, it's Candace. What's the guy's name?"

"Robert...uh...Binstock. Yeah, Binstock. Do you know him?"

Katherine leaned forward and Candace just shook her head. Robert was Candace's ex, and a world-class cheater who always came running back between women. Candace had to turn him down at least once a month, and apparently this was her lucky week.

"I'll be right there," she said, disconnecting the call with a sigh. "I guess I really do have to go. You'll be all right by yourself tonight?"

Katherine laughed. "It was just a vacation, *Candy.* I think I can handle it."

"Ugh. No matter how many times I tell him, it's always got to be shorter with him." She rose from the couch and Katherine followed her into the hall where she'd left her purse and jacket.

"Don't feel too bad," Katherine said. "David called me Kat. Said it suited my 'sensual' side better."

"That actually does make me feel better, in an odd sort of way." Candace opened the door and stepped outside. Katherine was surprised to see how dark it had gotten.

"Good luck with the guys," she said, trying unsuccessfully to stifle a grin. "Candy."

Her friend laughed. "Sleep well, Kat. I'll talk to you soon. If I survive the night."

Katherine waved and closed the door, locking it before she turned and saw her things in the hall where she'd dropped them. Briefly contemplating picking them up, she closed her eyes firmly and walked right by. They'd still be there in the morning, and she didn't have to work again until Monday. Plenty of time to do the cleaning, cooking and household chores.

Right now, she just wanted to go curl up in bed with a glass of wine and a good book for the rest of the night.

With any luck, she'd even be able to sleep.

Katherine tossed and turned, comfortable enough, but unable to settle in to sleep. It was almost worse now, because she knew what it felt like to be rested, and that just added to her stress at still being awake. Checking the clock, she groaned. Three in the morning. Maybe if she just got up and did something she'd be tired enough to close her eyes.

She went to the kitchen and poured herself a glass of milk, taking it into her office where the computer screen beckoned. She checked her email, deleting all the spam items. Only one message left, from an unfamiliar address. The subject simply read, "Kat."

Her fingers trembled as she clicked it open.

Kat,

I got your email address from your scuba reservation. There are things I wanted to tell you last night, apologies I wanted to make. I know it doesn't really matter now, but I wish things had ended differently, if they had to end.

I thought you might have trouble sleeping again at home, so I left something in your bag. I don't know if it will help or not, but it's worth a try.

If you want to talk, I'm here.

Sweet dreams,

David

Katherine got up and went to her bag, pulling things out and tossing them wherever until she found it. One of his shirts - just a plain black tee, but she held it up to her face and breathed in his scent, her eyes closing as her whole body relaxed.

Not even sparing a glance at the mess, she got up and went to the bedroom, pulling her own nightshirt off and slipping David's shirt over her head. Turning off the light, she slipped into bed and pulled the covers up, his masculine aroma surrounding her like incense as she closed her eyes and smiled.

When she opened her eyes again, daylight was peeking through her bedroom blinds. She yawned, stretched, and got up, folding David's shirt and placing it neatly under her pillow as she made the bed. A long, hot shower and a cup of coffee had her feeling...good, actually.

Picking up the clothes in the hall, she started the laundry, finished unpacking and put away her suitcase. Pouring another cup of coffee, she finally went into the office and sat at her computer, David's email staring back at her from hours before.

She put her fingers on the keyboard. What could she say to him? Thanks for the shirt, obviously, but there was still so much left unsaid, and maybe it should stay that way. Shouldn't it?

David,

I don't know how you knew, but thank you for the shirt. It was just what I needed last night.

Please don't feel that you owe me anything, certainly no apologies. Despite all the stuff we went through, I had some good times, and learned a lot about myself. Candace seems to think I made a lot of progress too.

I'm not sure what else to say. Everything seems so surreal, like a dream. I can't thank you enough for everything you did to help me. I'll never forget it - or you.

I guess that's it. I hope you're doing well.

Kat

She clicked the send button before she could talk herself out of it, feeling ridiculous for making such a big deal out of such a small gesture. But it wasn't, not really. Not to her.

Closing her email, she opened her calendar and began the familiar task of making a list for the day. She had a few more days off, and a few things she wanted to get done before the normal work routine began again. Her mind kept drifting back to the island, and especially to that last night with David, but she forced it aside. Everything would be easier if she could just get back into her normal routines.

It had to.

* * * *

David read her email for the fifth time in a row. Light enough on the surface, she was clearly appreciative, but there was more underneath. And the way she'd signed off as "Kat" - he knew that was important. The image of her sleeping in the shirt he'd sent with her was enough to make his jeans tighter than they ought to be.

Sitting back in his chair he shook his head and chuckled to himself. Who'd have thought he'd be sitting here analyzing a simple email from a woman he'd slept with exactly twice and known for all of a week?

More importantly, what was he going to do about it? He couldn't seem to get her out of his head. Her scent still clung to the clothes he'd worn the night before she left. And that look in her eyes when she said she couldn't stay would haunt him for a long time. She'd wanted to. So why had she left?

He leaned forward and clicked the reply button on her email.

Kat,

I'm glad the shirt helped - it's one of my favorites. I bet it looks a lot better on you than it ever did on me.

I don't think you ever told me where you work. What do you do?

David

His phone rang just as he hit send, and he checked the clock, swearing under his breath. Closing the laptop, he answered the call.

"Sorry Amy, I lost track of time. I'll be there in five minutes."

One last glance at the only link between him and the most intriguing woman he'd met in a long time, and he headed out the door.

"Are we gonna get sued?" Amy asked after he'd gotten the last of the divers off the boat later that afternoon. "Your latest conquest didn't seem all that happy when we finally got her back to shore, despite your little talk."

David got a mop and started cleaning the deck, enjoying the hot mid-day sun on his back. "I don't think so," he said, focusing on the job at hand. "She seemed...okay last time I talked to her." He glanced up briefly to see Amy's eyebrows raise.

"And when was that, exactly?"

He shrugged. "I got her email off the reservation form and we've exchanged a couple notes, is all."

"Uh-huh." Amy moved into his path, forcing him to stop. "What are you doing, David?"

"Cleaning up. What's it look like I'm doing?"

She rolled her eyes. "I mean with her. Kat. What are you doing? She's there, you're here...is there something else going on?"

"Maybe. Probably not." He looked out over the water, squinting at the bright light reflecting up. "Look, I don't know. I just...there's something, you know? And I can't seem to let it go, even though I know I should."

Amy watched him for a minute, and then laughed softly. "Oh man. You really don't know, do you? Dude, I think you're in love with this girl."

David shook his head. "I've known her for a week, Amy. And I don't even really know her. It's just lust, that's all. It'll wear off eventually."

She grinned. "Yeah. You just keep telling yourself that." Moving out of his way, she gathered her things. "I'm taking off. Two tours tomorrow, so if you could be on time..."

"I'll be here."

He finished swabbing the decks and made another trip through the boat to make sure everything was put away and locked up before he finally left for the night. When he got back to his room, he stood staring at his laptop on the table for a long moment.

Cold turkey was probably the best way to deal with the whole Kat situation. Getting to know her would just make it worse. It couldn't be love, not yet, and if he just cut himself off, everything would work itself out. She'd made her choice. Why should he put any more effort into a relationship? He didn't even want a relationship.

Right?

Determined, he left again, buying himself a quick dinner and then heading to the bar to scope out some local action. But nothing really caught his eye, and after a few beers he found himself back in his room, sitting at the table with another drink in hand as he contemplated the laptop again.

"Fuck," he murmured, kicking off his shoes and moving to the bed. She left. It was over. She probably wasn't even thinking of him. Tipping the bottle back, he finished it off and tossed it into the garbage before turning out the light. Sliding under the covers he closed his eyes.

And saw Kat in nothing but his shirt, beckoning with one finger and a smile.

* * * *

"David hasn't written back?" Candace laced her fingers together on her desk, her expression sympathetic, but firm.

Katherine shook her head. "No. And I don't want to bother him either. I don't know if it's the fact that I'm a professional organizer that put him off, or if he just decided he didn't want to talk anymore, but it doesn't matter. It's been two weeks. So I need...something. Please. I just need one night's sleep."

"We tried drugs already, Katherine - none of them helped except tranquilizers, and you can't take those for the rest of your life. I don't have anything else to give you. For some reason, David's scent helps you sleep. There's research out there that shows some people actually do get addicted to the hormones another person puts out around them. Unfortunately if he doesn't want to be around you, and you won't ask him for another shirt while we have a lab try to manufacture something synthetic to replace him, I'm really not sure what our options are."

"Okay." Katherine sighed, rubbing her head with one hand. "I'm sorry. I'm just tired, and I'm having trouble at work--"

"I know. I'm so sorry. I wish there was something I could do. Did you try the afternoon workouts?"

"I tried running, weight lifting and swimming. And I think it helps, but it's hard to keep it up when I'm so tired, you know? Catch-22 kind of thing."

Candace nodded. "Okay. Let me think about it for a day or so, and I'll figure something out, no matter what. There has to be some chemical that just isn't balanced in your body that's causing this, otherwise David's scent wouldn't work either. Can you hang in there through the weekend?"

"I don't have much choice, do I?" Katherine rose from her seat. "By the way, how's your house guest doing? Is he gone yet?"

A hot flush rose in Candace's cheeks, and Katherine grinned. "I guess not. Good for you. I'd say have a good weekend, but I suspect that's not going to be a problem. *Candy.*"

Her friend laughed. "Get out of here. Try to get some sleep. I'll call just as soon as I can."

Katherine winked, and then turned to go. She was nearly out the door when Candace called after her.

"Oh wait - Kat? What's the name of David's company? One of my clients is going down there next month, and wants to book a tour. I figured I'd send some business his way."

Katherine hesitated a moment before answering. "It's just called Deep Sea Tours. They have a web site." Then she walked out the door, an ache in the center of her chest that she didn't dare stop to analyze.

Chapter Eight

David closed his laptop with a sigh. Hard as he'd tried, two weeks hadn't been enough to get Kat off his mind, and now he wasn't sure what to think. Dr. Candace Wilson seemed to think that the only way Katherine could get a good night's sleep was with David's scent, and she'd implied that while a shirt would do, his entire self would be better.

She'd even gone so far to imply that if Kat was doing poorly without him, he was probably in bad shape without her too. Apparently there was some chemical reaction between some people where they actually got addicted to each other. A scary thought, but it did make sense in a twisted sort of way.

He glanced over at the empties littering his nightstand. The doc would probably have a field day with that.

He picked up his cell phone and dialed Amy's number.

"What would you say if I quit?"

She laughed. "About time. Hey David?"

"Yeah?"

"Have a nice flight."

He disconnected the call and reached for a beer, contemplating the label for a long moment. Setting it back down, he got up and started to pack.

* * * *

Corkscrew in hand, Katherine contemplated the bottle of wine on the counter. The clock on the microwave said it was nearly one in the morning, and as if on cue, she yawned.

She'd used alcohol to knock herself out a few times, but it took a whole bottle and the hangover generally wasn't worth it. Tomorrow was Sunday though, and considering that the only other option seemed to be tossing and turning until the sun came up, a hangover actually didn't sound too bad. At least she'd be rested. Sort of.

Resigned, she reached for the bottle and poised the tip of the corkscrew over the cork.

The doorbell rang. She dropped the corkscrew.

She didn't know anyone who would drop by at this hour without an emergency, and she was half-way to the door before it occurred to her that it could be a

her in close to his body and pulled the covers up over them both.

"I can't believe you're here," she said, running her fingers down his chest. "I thought--"

"Shhh..." He held a finger to her lips, and then replaced it with a kiss. "Sleep first. Then we'll talk, okay?"

She smiled, pressing her lips to the hard plane of his chest and then closed her eyes.

* * * *

Warm, soft kisses moving slowly down her spine made Katherine moan with pleasure some time later. Was she dreaming? She didn't want to open her eyes and find out. Strong hands caressed her ribs, her hips, her thighs, just before teeth nipped gently at one side of her rear.

She yelped, not in pain but in surprise, rewarded with a deep chuckle from under the covers as she rolled to her back.

Images flashed through her mind - David coming through the door, carrying her to bed, surrounding her with his body as well as his scent.

He was really here. Under her covers, and from the feel of things, about to make her feel even better than a decent night's sleep already had.

Hot lips scorched a path up one thigh as his hands gently pried her legs apart. He touched his tongue to her core and she arched up, the sensation catching her off guard and sending tingles of pleasure racing through her body. Just the right pressure in all the right spots had her panting and whimpering, completely at his mercy and loving every second of it.

She was on the brink, her body wound tight when he crawled up and swirled his tongue around one pert nipple, then the other. One long thrust and he filled her, sparking her release with his total possession of her body.

Her mind went blank, the world a fog as she floated on a cloud of ecstasy. It felt like a long time before she could even open her eyes, locking into David's intense stare the moment she could focus.

"You are so beautiful," he said, drawing his hips back slightly and sliding forward again. "I don't know why or how, or even if it's love or not, but I can't live without you, Kat. You're part of me."

He kept up his slow, lazy strokes, driving her crazy as she lifted a hand to caress the side of his face. "I can't live without you either. I think we're stuck with each other. If that doesn't define love, I don't know what does."

He nodded, leaning in for a kiss. Then another, and another as he stroked her harder, faster. That delicious pressure radiated out from her core and she urged him on, holding her own pleasure off until his arms began to shake and he thrust one more hard, glorious time. Arching into him again she squeezed him with her inner muscles and let go, welcoming the flow of energy that seemed to envelope them both.

She felt empty when he finally rolled away, but he pulled her along, her front to his back, his arm over her torso and one leg over both of hers. She felt safe, cocooned in his embrace.

Loved.

"David?"

"Yes Kat?" He kissed her shoulder.

"How long can you stay?" She held her breath.

"Forever."

The word rumbled through her like a freight train, shaking her to the core like nothing ever had before. His grip on her tightened, and she snuggled as close against him as she could. This. This is what she'd been missing all along.

"Sleep with me?"

"Always."

About the Author

A full-time webmistress by day, Jamie DeBree writes steamy, action-packed romantic suspense and contemporary romance late into the night. Her goal is to create the perfect blend of sensual attraction, emotional tension and fast-paced adventure, similar to the television crime dramas she's hopelessly addicted to.

Born in Billings Montana, she resides there with her husband and two over-sized lap dogs. She reads in a wide variety of genres including romance, erotica, action/adventure, thriller, horror and literary fiction.

For information on upcoming books, visit jamiedebree.com.